BEAUTIFUL ATROCITIES

ROSS JEFFERY

FOREWORD BY
ERIC LAROCCA

CONTENT WARNING

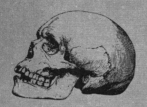

It is never my intention to offend my readers with the stories I write.

I have put a list of content warnings and possible triggers in the back of the book which you can find on page 168 if needed.

Many of the content warnings are never overtly shown on the page, but I feel it is my duty to inform you of these themes before you dive in.

But this is a horror collection and so at the end of the day I hope it leaves you horrified.

Also by Ross Jeffery

Juniper

Tome

Scorched

Tethered

Only The Stains Remain

Milk Kisses and Other Stories

First published in Great Britain in 2022.

CEMETERY GATES MEDIA

Copyright © Ross Jeffery 2021

Ross Jeffery has asserted his right under the Copyright, Designs and Patents Act 1988 to be identified as the author of this work.

The Great Withering 2021 - Hex-Periments (first published)

ISBN: 9798416655389

Header Image by Gordon Johnson (Pixabay).

Cover Art by Prettysleepy Art (Pixabay).

Cover Design by Tomek Dzido.

Formatting by Ross Jeffery.

FOREWORD

BY ERIC LAROCCA

Like many of the talented authors I was privileged enough to interact with throughout the course of the Covid-19 pandemic, I came to know author Ross Jeffery through social media after he kindly reviewed one of my novellas, *Starving Ghosts in Every Thread*. Eager to connect with more writers (*despite the fact we were separated by thousands of miles and a major ocean*), Ross and I quickly became friends, and he was kind enough to send me a care package containing his previously published work.

The first interaction I had with Ross's work was his Bram Stoker nominated novel, *Tome*. Of course, I anticipated that the novel would be of a certain quality given the fact that most people in the horror community on Twitter and Instagram were raving about the book; however, I certainly could have never expected Ross's skillful command of language, his visceral descriptions, his expert building and efficient sustaining of dread. I found myself mesmerized by his writing and knew full well I had to consume everything the man had ever written, truly believing that I was playing witness to the birth of a master talent.

Of course, I was smitten with the idea of crafting a foreword to

Ross' short story collection, *Beautiful Atrocities*. It was an honor I scarcely considered myself worthy of; however, I'll do my best to provide a cogent and compelling introduction before you, dear reader, embark on a journey into the heart of depravity.

When pondering how to best introduce this collection to the unsuspecting reader, I considered going through each story collected and analyzing the themes and motifs present. However, as I considered this further, I realized that I want the reader to approach the collection with the same uncertainty, the same ambiguity that I had possessed when Ross first sent me the stories for my consideration. I think there's something to be said for "less is more" in the horror genre. The less you know, the better.

As I continued to ponder how to introduce this collection, I considered the word "atrocities." Like most words in the English language, the word has Latin roots and more directly comes from the French word: *atrocité*. The original Latin word (*atrocitas*) simply means "cruel." Discovering the etymology of this word made me ruminate on the stories of the collection and made me realize that there is certainly a theme of cruelty running throughout each of the tales Ross has collected here. It's the cruelty of humanity—the mercilessness that a parent might impose on their child, the viciousness that lovers might inflict upon one another in a moment of gentleness.

Even though most of the stories contained in this collection deal with cruelty in some form, one must not forget the importance of the word "beauty" when coupled with the word "cruelty." Ross executes these moments of barbarity, of viciousness, of unbridled depravity with the tenderness and care of an accomplished surgeon. Of course, this unique coupling of "beauty" and "cruelty" conjures the likes of writers who have dabbled in the area before with uncompromising skill and verve. I think of authors such as Clive Barker or Michael McDowell—veterans of the grotesquely beautiful horror, writers who conjured the most horrific and unsettling images and rendered them as things of beauty.

Whether it's the visceral uneasiness permeating throughout the story "One Piece Remains" or the unrestrained debauchery show-cased in the tale "<TheCollectorofRuinedThings>" Ross Jeffery skill-fully illustrates how beauty and cruelty are interconnected and rightfully so.

Beautiful Atrocities will test your comfort, dear reader, and will beguile and mystify you as you come to question whether beauty or cruelty has revealed itself to you. As you read each of the stories in the collection, you will come to understand how beauty and cruelty are dovetailed and interwoven in a unique way.

Like most of his captivating and exceptional writing, Ross shows us how there's magnificence to be found in anguish, just as there's misery to be found in splendor.

Eric LaRocca
Boston, MA
October 2021

ONE PIECE REMAINS

The package arrives the same time each week. Every Thursday. 11:42pm.

I sit on the sofa. My wife's lying down and peace reigns for a short while.

The bottle of beer is cold and condensation bleeds down the bottle; trickling through my fingers where it dampens my knee. When I lift the bottle to take a swig, I notice the rounded watermark of its base imprinted on my jeans. Thank goodness I didn't put it on the coffee table. The ring it would leave, the irritation it would have caused my wife, followed by her incessant need to buff and polish that ring out of existence would have taken over, as if it's eradication would give her a meaning to exist for a few short moments as she'd go about her work diligently and frenzied.

I gulp down the remaining liquid, the coolness thirst quenching and exactly what I need.

I suddenly hear the unmistakable footfall of our visitor emanating from the outside hallway. My eyes flick to the door as I listen intently at the placing of one foot, followed by the dragging of their trailing leg. I don't stand, don't go to the door or attempt to peer out through the spy hole at the elusive figure that brings our weekly treat, the unknown entity that showers us with offerings from their toil.

I wonder what they'll bring this week?

I imagine the figure shambling down the corridor, a lumbering Quasimodo like being. They always come at this hour, as the day is dying but before the birth of the next. A practiced ritual, one that I've grown to love and look forward to. It's taken time however to adore these awful moments, but as it nears its inevitable completion I never want it to end because it's given me a sense of purpose.

I've no idea how many more packages remain, surely they must be running out of things to send. I guess that's a worry for another day.

The light beneath the front door darkens. I edge forwards, anxious to stand, but if I do and they find out they might go back on our original deal, so I remain seated; fidgeting in my own flesh. My knees bounce up and down, my fingers knit together in a latticework of eager flesh and raw emotions. My jaw's clenched so tight my fillings ache in their gummy moorings. I'm sweaty and panting, every inch an addict awaiting their next fix, their liquid oblivion, their smoke-filled suicide.

I yearn with an insatiable hunger to see what they've brought me tonight, but I must wait because all good things come to those who do.

I hear the ragged breaths of the courier on the other side of the door. A smoker by my guess as he wheezes and splutters through his task, the sound of an emphysema patient nearing an empty tank. The light soon returns under the door and in the middle of that horizontal beam is a black void.

Our latest gift and their most recent offering.

There's a noise from within the apartment. My eyes flit around our sparse dwelling, from cobweb to cobweb, light fitting to ceiling rose. I scan each crack that snakes the walls, each fissure a glaring reminder of how much time has passed, and how little we still have to offer.

Has my wife awoken so soon from her slumber?

I rubbish the thought as quickly as it arrives as I know she's lying down, resting and recuperating. She needs her rest now more than ever. She sleeps like the dead since this long-suffering nightmare began. I only wish I could join her in her oblivion, but I have to stay awake, to receive what they send. The boiler roars to life and I realise that the previous sound was just the pipes behind the plasterboard groaning like bodies interned in the ground.

The nights of their delivery are a solitary affair where I sit alone and contemplate our fate. If only we had the money they thought we had. If we did, this whole sorry ordeal might have worked out differently.

If we were rich we wouldn't be in this predicament. We wouldn't be piecing our life back together one macabre offering at a time.

They took her and then demanded £20,000 for her safe return. We didn't have a pot to piss in and I briefly thought that they should have done their homework; because they'd have quickly realised my wife was an underpaid teacher, and I was let go from my job in the wake of Covid. We scrimp and save but at the end of each month we just have enough to survive, to keep our heads above the undertow of life which pulls at our trailing legs, threatening to pull us down to the watery depths below.

They didn't listen and failed to understand the gravity of our situation; quite frankly, they just didn't care.

They still wanted the cash and their greed made them blind to the fact we just couldn't acquire it. Banks would never loan us the money and there wasn't even a chance we could beg for it because we were well and truly in the red. Our finances were reflected on our bank statements as mortal wounds each month, we just couldn't pay them what they wanted.

A week later, after the realisation of our fiscal plight had thrown a spanner in their plans the first package arrived.

There have been sixty-two packages since, spanning two years. Each package varies in size, weight, shape and form. Some were tubular, deftly wrapped in brown paper and string. Reminiscent of a prime cuts of meat from *'The Hook and Cleaver'*, the artisan butcher's shop around the corner. Some were dropped off in boxes, large square ones that you'd get from Amazon that were always too roomy for the things they contained. Then came a smattering of smaller jewellery sized boxes. One thing was clear through all this torture, whatever the size and shape, they took great delight in their work and the horrors their hands had crafted.

They found great satisfaction in their maltreatment of us.

The door to our block slams closed. I listen intently and decipher our messenger's ungainly shuffle heading away from our building through the open window. I stand but dare not glance outside. After his car drives away, I step sluggishly to the door, ready to discover their weekly offering.

I place the box on the table next to my empty bottle before sitting to inspect the package. It's fairly small, the size of a shoebox, a string tied into a bow adorns the top. I scan the box, spin it slowly on the table. I stop its rotation when I notice one of the corners has a greasy darkened smear, the brown paper turned a rusted-red like the leaves in autumn. It's only located in this corner and so assume the stain emanates from within, a tiny hint at the grisly morsel it contains.

I lean forward, pinch the string of the bow and pull. I quickly tear at paper, desperate to get to the good stuff like a kid at Christmas.

Taking hold of the lid, I lift it slowly and peer inside.

Atop the coiled flesh inside is a blood-smeared note. The meat it balances on arranged like a bird's nest. I pluck it from its crimson niche and discover to my surprise a dark void it was hiding. In the centre of the nest are a collection of teeth; molars, premolars, incisors, and canines — each shining like enamelled eggs. I would have shuddered at this type of discovery before, as I had with the earlier packages, but now I've become accustomed to the macabre; desensitised by the violence. Now, after so long, it's just another day and another step closer to finally having her home.

Pulling my eyes away from the gore I decide to inspect the card. Turning it over reveals a hand scrawled message on the reverse, a first since they started sending these awful packages. I read it, then read it again. Realisation strikes home and panic becomes a knife slipped between my ribs, robbing me of my breath.

One piece remains.

I throw the card into the box, close the lid and carry it under my arm to my wife. She'll want to know this ordeal is nearly at an end. We almost have her back. In pieces. Home at last. I rush down the corridor to where she's lying down. Bursting into the room I find her where I left her, sleeping like the dead.

"It's here, it's here," I exclaim, giddy with excitement as I place the box on the bedside table.

"Guess what they sent this time?" I turn to her, realising that she couldn't answer me even if she wanted to.

"Right..." I feign surprise and hit myself on the head with my palm. "Silly me, I forgot. It's impossible to speak without a tongue isn't it dear? Well, you're in luck, they sent it back!"

I lift the lid and remove the coiled organ. Teeth sticking to its long, slick form. Stroking at the cold meat with my other hand I manage to dislodge the teeth, each falling into the box with a clatter, a macabre confetti raining down in small thuds.

Shuffling over to my wife I then kneel beside her on the carpet. Dampness seeps through my jeans as a noisome reek blooms from the rancid carpet causing me to gag. I lay the tongue on the blackened, dried husk of her body before taking hold of her jaw with my outstretched hands.

I prise her rusted maw open, the dried joints of her jaw squeak as I force it wider; bone rubbing on bone, no supple tissue remain to aid in the process. When her mouth's finally open I begin to feed her the tongue, sliding the cold flesh down her gullet a centimetre at a time. Her gaping mouth ingests the organ like a sword swallower would their tools of the trade. Her throat becomes engorged as I ram the tongue back from where it came, there's resistance at first but her body soon begins to accept the foreign entity and she swallows it down.

"I can tell you're happy about that, but I want to put that smile back on your face. You're almost home darling!"

The teeth clatter within the box like errant coins in a tramp's tin cup as I bring it closer. I place the box onto the ever-expanding dark ring that circles her body. I couch down and grab a handful of her teeth and begin to examine them on my palm. Picking one from the harvest I start the painstaking job of piecing her smile back together. The holes from where her teeth were originally extracted are still visible, little sunken indents in her blackened gums.

After a few botched attempts I finally have them all back in their moorings. It's not the neatest of smiles, but it gives her face a bit of structure at least, brightening the black hole that had become her mouth.

"There's only one parcel left. They was a note this time. It said one piece remains... and we both know what that is don't we? Soon we'll be together again, like it was before."

Gazing down at the jigsaw her body's become I can't help but smile at my handiwork. Each piece of her is back where it should be but she's far from connected. There's the noticeable absence of tissue, sinew and bone that would normally tether each limb to the whole being. Each part of her sits roughly where it should, but in all honesty she's a crazy paving of the human form.

I sit down beside her and place my hand on her shrunken chest. My fingers play with a flap of skin on her chest, a hole I can't wait to fill.

I lift the parchment-like skin and stare into the vacant cavity where her heart should be.

"Soon." I whisper, but my love doesn't answer.

WHEN IT IS TRULY TIME

R uth sits in her usual spot by the window with a view of the front lawn.

The sun streams in through the lead-lined glass, casting shadows like prison bars across the floorboards and the inhabitants of the room. Taking in the sight she smiles to herself.

"We're all prisoners to something." She whispers softly, quietly enough that no one hears, but loud enough to mean something; to her at least.

She reclines back into the comfortable wingback chair. Her gaze soon returns to the outside world, revealing the luscious green lawn and people coming and going from the facility, each seemingly living their lives to the full.

The leather of the chair has become moulded to her over time, like the countless other chairs and souls that have found their way to this godawful place. The armrests are cracked like old skin, where eager and often pained hands have strangled the leather during their treatments; Ruth's fingers have gripped them too from time-to-time, it's one of the only way to fight the agony.

Pain lives here and so does its children – discomfort and sorrow.

Her eyes rove over the other people waiting – all sickly speci-
mens. Each at the end of their own ropes. The frail old lady sitting
three seats over is just a bag of bones covered in a doily of flesh. Her
skin has that jaundice look of the terminally ill, but the woman's
smile – Ruth notices – brings a much-needed sense of life to this
place of death. It's angelic and hurts Ruth to gaze any longer,
because she suddenly feels the sharp sting of her own fragility of life,
and the emptiness that awaits her once she leaves this room.

Ruth glances at the woman's stick-thin and liver-spotted arm,
notices the tube that's connected by a needle into the aggravated
skin at the crook of the woman's elbow. Ruth's fingers find her own
bruised entry site. Her digits begin to meander over the place of
pain and pleasure and she realises that she'll miss it when it's all
over, when there's no more needles and no more treatments.
Glancing up to the bag of cloudy fluid hanging above the old
woman's chair Ruth's stomach begins to flutter; knowing that her
time and bag will arrive soon enough. The nurse will poke and prod
and slip the needle deep, there will be pain, but there will also be
utter bliss.

Turning her head to the side she glances down the large sterile
room. She counts seven people, seven souls adrift in this ward. Each
of them alone. Each awaiting or already partaking in their treatments. All wanting to feel something other than the pain that
presides over their sorrow-filled bodies.

How many other rooms are dotted around this facility?

The thought scares her. She doesn't really want to know, because
if she does, she'll realise that there are more than those assembled
here; alone, lost, and hanging on to that last glimmer of hope, until
it's snuffed out and they're forced to face the cruel hand they've been
dealt.

Reaching out she grasps a glass of water from the table next to
her chair. They insist that patients drink, keep their fluids up and
Ruth is a stickler for the rules and so she drinks. After her first treatment she soon realised what happened if you didn't follow the rules;

the pain and discomfort that followed that first appointment was a special kind of hell.

She lifts the cup to her mouth now and drinks greedily at the cool liquid within. The water quenching the thirst she hadn't realised she'd possessed.

Placing the cup down her eyes scan the room again and she notices some familiar friends, people she's journeyed this dark path with. It's always hard to wait your turn, and the blessed relief that comes from the sharp end of a needle. But she must. There's a routine, a strange protocol that needs to be followed, and so she enjoys and endures this moment of voyeurism whilst it lasts. She takes great delight in seeing these haunted souls finding a momentary peace from their pain and she's buoyed by the fact that she'll soon join them in their sweet oblivion.

There are other souls she doesn't recognise. Strangers which have taken the places of her previous acquaintances who it would appear have left this place for pastures new.

The newcomers wear masks of fear and trepidation, some even look guilty, almost afraid of what's to come and what they'll have to face in this place of sorrow. Ruth wants to reach out a hand to comfort them in their hour of distress, but that's strictly against the rules. *Contamination* they'd said. Only the nurses are allowed to touch the patients. And so, Ruth sits and observes their quiet suffering, knowing that she was once like them, at the start of her treatment. She hasn't the heart to tell them it doesn't get any easier.

It was the great unknown that scared her the most.

Ruth had spoken to a few friends that had come here for their treatments, each suffering like she had. They'd mentioned that a deep-rooted sickness always followed the treatments, a ghastly ailment that made you want to die. They'd said that her skin would feel as if it were on fire, so much so that she'd want to claw deep furrows in her flesh just to let the pain dribble out. They said her joints would ache as if each limb were near dislocation and that she'd suffer night sweats which would leave her sheets slick with the poison they'd pumped into her. They were right, Ruth had suffered greatly; but she knew the worst was yet to come.

It gets better she wanted to say to those hopeless souls gawking at their new environment, but she knew it would be a terrible lie and so instead she bites her tongue as everyone does; because each person here is suffering in a deeply personal way.

Ruth won't be here after today to hold their hand even if she was allowed. The nurse informed her when she checked in that today would be her last treatment and she was deeply saddened by the news.

How can it be over already?

The prospect of not coming back, of saying goodbye, was the worst kind of pain imaginable. This place had become somewhat of a home to her over the last few months, a place to belong among strangers and grieve the circumstances and troubles of her life. But she understands clearly why she must leave, why she must say good-bye; because there will be nothing left for her here, not after they pump her full of her final dose.

Ruth glances down the hall, a young bald man sits a few seats over. The veins on his scalp are prominent, as if worms were crawling beneath his skin. She notices him muttering, plugged into his bag and receiving his treatment. His hands gesticulate as if he's caressing someone's face that he deeply cared for; but there's no one there, there never is. She tries to make out the quiet lament on his lips, but all she can hear is the nurse's rubber-soled shoes squeaking their way towards her.

Ruth peers over to the young girl opposite. A look of fatigue has removed any essence of youth from her face. *So young* Ruth muses, noticing the drip in her arm before carrying on her train of thought. *What burdens must she be carrying. It's not right for a child to be surrounded by so much death.*

Ruth watches on as the girl's eyes rise to meet her gaze. They share a glance, a connection. They're instantly bound together in that moment, not in ways of this world but in the one that awaits us all at the end. Both are tethered to this reality but desperate to be released into the next. Ruth smiles. To her surprise the girl smiles back and between the gaps from the girl's missing teeth Ruth notices a blistered tongue; a common side effect. The girl winces at the pain her smile brings, and her sad, empty eyes flick to the vacant bag hanging above her as a tear escapes her eye before running down her cheek. It becomes clear to both of them that the girl's time here has come to an end.

Everyone cries at the end.

The nurse stops in front of Ruth, obscuring the crying girl and severing the momentary connection they'd shared. Staring up at the burly nurse Ruth smiles coyly before relaxing back into her chair and allowing the nurse to hook her up.

Ruth watches the nurse fuss with the container, which appears to be running on fumes, and from what Ruth's seen and heard the final drops are the most potent; as if the dregs of her treatment have fermented and grown crueller over time.

"So, this is your final dose," the nurse says, trying to put Ruth at ease but failing greatly.

Ruth nods, fighting back tears. If she speaks she knows that she'll cry and she isn't ready for that, yet.

"Well, let's get you all set up and then I'll leave you be."

Ruth peers to her left, the drip stand hangs over her like a metallic gallows, which it is in a way; torture of the worst possible kind, but it's almost over. The smiley nurse hooks the bag onto the hanger and uncoils the wire, the needle is still sheathed at the business end. Ruth watches the pitiful contents settle in the bag before the nurse grips her arm and begins to roll it over, exposing the tender underside. Old bruises decorate the crook of her elbow, denoting the passage of time and her previous treatments. Each bruise a painful reminder that time is running out and she's utterly powerless to stop it.

Ruth looks away as the nurse unsheathes the needle, she's never liked injections and this one she especially despises. The nurse gropes at her bruised arm, fingers tapping and pulling the skin taut, desperately seeking the vein she needs to fill.

"Just a little scratch," the nurse purrs sweetly.

Ruth feels the needle bite, hears tape being torn and squirms in her seat as the needle is retracted, the catheter plugged into her vein as the tube is taped securely to her arm. Ruth glances up at the nurse who's fiddling with the roller clamp. After she's satisfied with its position the nurse observes the contents of the bag as it begins to float down into the drip chamber.

"There's not much left," the nurse says softly, before jiggling the bag slightly; encouraging the stubborn substance to slide down the tube.

"Just be prepared, this last bit hurts like nothing you've ever felt. Just thought I'd forewarn you... you're all set to go. Are you ready?"

Ruth nods. She doesn't trust her voice this close to the end.

The nurse clicks the valve open before scurrying off to her other patients. Ruth becomes lost in her own thoughts as she waits for the sting that's accompanied her previous procedures, but it doesn't arrive when it should. She turns her gaze to the bag and reads the label affixed to the top.

DONOR: Ruby Miles (Daughter)
AQUIRED: 12/06/2006
PATIENT: Ruth Miles (Mother)
PATIENT DOB: 14/08/1982
CONTENTS TO BE CONSUMED NO LATER THAN THREE MONTHS
AFTER FIRST SESSION.

Ruth glances down from the stinging reminder. The foggy substance trapped within cascades into the drip tube like smoke. Turning her attention to the plastic cable that leads to the catheter in her arm she's watches on as the ghost of her daughter creeps along the tube, slowly snaking its way towards her arm.

She'll soon be reunited with her daughter and they'll share one body again. She'll hear her daughter's voice for the last time, because after today, there will be no more solution. Her daughter's ghost will be used up, gone forever; and Ruth will be truly alone.

The ghost in the tube inches closer to the catheter as if drawn to the vein that will carry it to Ruth's heart and brain, where she'll live again for mere moments. Ruth hopes that those final precious memories will last a lifetime. She turns her eyes away from the tube, stares out the window and waits patiently to be greeted by her daughter's voice one last time.

When it is truly time, are any of us ready to say goodbye? Ruth muses as she prepares for her daughter's swansong.

Pain rips through her arm as her daughter's ghost announces its arrival and finally enters her bloodstream. The pain quickly subsides and is replaced by the creeping sensation of anaesthetic which dances its way up to her neck. Her gaze is pulled from the window as a calming numbness hits her brain.

Ruth's eyes suddenly focus on her daughter who's now standing before her, alive.

"Will you stay a while mummy?"

Her daughter's voice pierces Ruth's heart afresh, paining her gravely in knowing that after today she'll never hear it as clearly as she does now. Maybe in time she'll even forget her daughter's little lisp and the slight inflection of her words.

"Of course my darling," Ruth replies as tears begin to blossom in her eyes, each tear a petal which falls in sorrow of what is to come.

"I'm scared," Ruby utters with a quivering lip as she steps closer; placing a hand in her mother's outstretched palm.

"So am I," Ruth manages to say as she grips her daughter's hand tightly, never wanting to let it go but knowing in time she must.

"Why don't we be scared together."

THE COLLECTOR OF RUINED THINGS

I do my best work at night.

Some people would call me a thief, I'd call myself a collector and distributor. The things I find I never keep for long, in fact, they pass through my hands like sand. It's strange what people request, peculiar what fetches a pretty penny, different strokes for different folks I guess, but people want what they want and I try to provide what I can, when I can.

My job doesn't afford me the luxury of friends or time to acquire them. It's quite a lonely existence - the graveyard shift, but I enjoy the quiet it affords me. When everyone else is tucked safely in bed and sleeping like the dead, I'm at work, cataloguing and moving things around. I don't mind the lonely existence. I was never good at talking to people anyway.

My little hobby started with pilfering things that people wouldn't miss. Under the cover of darkness, in the silence of the night I'd find myself standing over them, staring down whilst they slept, eyes closed, bodies still. They're always completely unaware I'm only inches from their faces, breathing heavily as my fingers rifled through their personal affects.

I'd pinched many things spanning a good many years; spectacles, pocket watches, necklaces, designer shoes and sometimes even cash. It was pocket change mostly, but on a good day, I'd find a money clip.

Stealing (or as I like to call it borrowing) wasn't exactly hard, it was child's play.

People don't realise how truly vulnerable they are while they're sleeping, believing they're safe and secure in the land of the dead; I never fear they'd wake and I guess that's what emboldened me. I became carefree, wanting to take more and more.

Tonight's item however could get me into a whole lot of trouble. It's a lot more than I usually take, and trust me, they're going to miss what I'm about to borrow.

There are a lot of sick people out there. Many I've come to find are sicker than I. Many of these sickos have become my customers, acquaintances and dare I even say it, *friends*?

These faceless *friends* collect peculiar things, oddities to feed their strange fetishes, and after a few months of dabbling on the Dark Web and a site called *SinBay,* I'd found something akin to a community. A place to belong in a world I felt I didn't.

It kept me occupied when I should have been working. I'd never known I could make money with the things I'd collected, but I did, I have, and I can't stop now. It's become somewhat an addiction. I've been able to turn this hobby into something of a career; a sick and twisted one at that, but it pays the bills and it's a whole lot easier than my real job. It's no wonder people turn to a life of crime when the pull of it is so alluring, the money so rewarding, and of course the stakes – so high.

If you could bottle this feeling I'm sure people would buy it to shoot into their veins.

I'd found that my tenement was the best place to start. I knew all the residents, not by name but by what they looked like; although finding a name is easy when you know where to look. Crumpled birth certificates, driver's licences, bank cards – everything's to hand if you have the time and inclination. It all started with Dorothy Peters, the eighty-seven-year-old from number 7.

I'd had a peculiar request from a user called **NailBiter97** (*to think there were possibly another 96 other nailbiters out there made me feel a little peculiar*).

With their order logged I set about acquiring the requested items. Holding the cold handle to Mrs. Peters door within my grasp and ensuring no one was watching I pulled the handle down and it clicked open. She was still. Silent. They're always so peaceful when I visit. I stared at her for a while, that frail body under her sheet, completely unaware.

I lifted the cover slowly to expose her feet. They were arthritic, the toes curled into themselves like gnarled roots. It was going to be a task to get what I needed, but I'd take my time and make the harvest. I slowly and delicately clipped her toenails; they were harder than I thought, thick and yellowed, but I persisted. The sound of the clippers shockingly loud, but she remained oblivious throughout. I retrieved the discoloured crescents, putting them all in a jar before I left.

I sold those nine toenails for £38.00 – and would have gotten more had I been able to get all ten, but her pinkie toe on her right foot was so malformed I couldn't prise it away from the others. I was ecstatic, £38.00 was a great haul for something people normally threw away.

The next request was from **IChewHair**, but there was a stipulation to this one; it had to be from a young girl. I had a limited pool of resources given my tenement so I settled for Jessica Day from number 12. Again I let myself in under the cover of darkness. I crept up on her slowly, and as I gazed down I found her looking like a china doll. I reached out and ran her blonde locks between my fingers which stirred up the scent of strawberries and coconut. Her hair felt wiry under my fingers, dead. Wait, isn't all hair dead? It doesn't feel pain, doesn't scream out when it's cut; only when you yank it from the root do you feel the pain.

And so, with a tuft of her hair in my hand I snipped it slowly, the slicing of follicles louder than I anticipated. It sounded as if I were cutting fabric, but she remained still. I've become good at not being noticed. I'd managed to sell that clump of hair for £100.00 after telling **IChewHair** she was seventeen (*I'd included a photo of her driver's licence for proof*). They'd said that she was too old for top shelf payment which could have quadrupled my payload. I'd thought about not sending it, that I'd find a better buyer, but £100.00 was a £100.00 and so I sent it, there were plenty more dolls on the shelf if I needed them.

Soon after, another request came through SinBay from **IPFreely**. They said they knew someone from my tenement, and that this request was personal. They'd been bullied by this guy years back and well, **IPFreely** wanted something from the now middle-aged prick to help him with closure. Jacob Harper was the pricks name, from number 22. He'd only moved in a few days ago and I didn't know much about him, but that didn't put me off. In a supply and demand culture I needed to get the customer **IPFreely** what he demanded and I wasn't about to wait around and get to know the guy before pilfering his personal affects.

I stood above Jacob, his torso muscular and ripped, after much time spent in the gym. His body was indeed a temple, one I was going to ransack. I touched his chest, my fingers danced over the contours of his muscles. My fingers soon skated down to his hand; it was the rings I was after. Each finger was bejewelled with signets and sovereigns. **IPFreely** only wanted one, but whilst I was there I'd take the lot. Unfortunately they wouldn't budge. I pulled but they'd all become lodged behind thick knuckles, stooping low I placed a cold, meaty finger in my mouth and sucked. I lubricated the digit until the ring slipped off. He slept through the whole sorry scene, my entire hand-fellatio performance went unnoticed. I sold the one with the initials JH for £360.00 to **IPFreely** and kept the others.

Nothing gets the heart rate pumping and the comments flying on SinBay more than a semi naked photograph of a young woman. I'd shared a photo from one of my late night prowls. It was the girl from number 13, Mariah Serenova. She was laying there in her pink panties and brassiere which contrasted boldly against her porcelain completion. I felt bad about putting the picture online without her consent, but that feeling didn't last for long; not after I saw how much people were willing to pay for her silky garments. The only proviso the bidders had is that it had to be those exact items. They had to be worn and dirty, soiled would be best they'd said. There were some sick people out there and I was their methadone. The bidding peaked at £1000.00 it could have gone higher, what with her being a petite little thing and not some old heifer selling her grubby wears for bingo money (*there were a load of those on SinBay*).

I returned the following night to fulfil the order for **RabbitGirl69**. Mariah's knickers came off slowly as I slid them down her long legs and hooked them off her feet. As I peered up at her prone body the blonde thatch of hair between her legs seemed to glisten in the light as if tiny crystals had been threaded into her pubic hair. My buyer would be happy. I moved to the side and used a pair of scissors to cut the bra free. I didn't want to manhandle her more than necessary, because at the end of the day I'm not a monster, I'm just trying to make ends meet. I snipped the straps and cut the middle band between the cups before pulling it out from under her resting body. She never made a sound (they never make a sound). I've become a ghost; a living, breathing, money making phantom of the night.

Tonight, I'll be making a killing because £10,000.00 is a lot of money however you slice it.

FistPumpDallas messaged me privately; they obviously didn't want their request appearing on any messaging board for the world to see and screenshot, so they slipped into my DM's.

<FistPumpDallas> Do you do requests?
<TheCollectorOFRuinedThings> Yes. What is it you're after?
<FistPumpDallas> A hand.

<TheCollectorOFRuinedThings > A hand with what? I don't do that kinda stuff.

<FistPumpDallas> No. I want a hand. Fingers. Palm. Wrist.

<TheCollectorOFRuinedThings> Okay. I may be able to help.

<FistPumpDallas> Good.

<TheCollectorOFRuinedThings> Male or Female? Young or old?

<FistPumpDallas> Not bothered by age. Female (MUST). Paint nails black before sending.

<TheCollectorOFRuinedThings> Sorry to be crude but how much are you offering?

<TheCollectorOFRuinedThings> This is a delicate acquisition as I'm sure you are aware.

<FistPumpDallas> £10,000.00 if you can ensure speedy secured delivery.

<TheCollectorOFRuinedThings> Order confirmed. I will message when acquired for shipping details.

<FistPumpDallas> First half of money sent to your *<TheCollectorOfRuinedThings>* user account. So you know I am serious about our deal.

<TheCollectorOFRuinedThings> Thank you. But you didn't need to do that – I've not acquired it yet.

<FistPumpDallas> You will.

So, tonight will be my Burke and Hare moment.

Body parts had just become the new must have on *SinBay*.

I made my way to her dwelling, number four. She'd arrived a few days ago but I still didn't know her name. I don't think anyone does. She'd arrived the same day as that prick Jacob Harper. Just thinking about him makes my throat tighten, as if I can still taste his foul cold fingers in my mouth. I grip the handle to her door pull it open gently. The metallic door swings wide and I reach inside to grab the metal slab and begin to slide her out. The shelf glides effortlessly on the rubber rollers, her body covered by an eggshell blue sheet like all the others before her.

I peer over my shoulder to check that we're alone. There's never anyone here, but it's wise to remain vigilant. If you don't, that's how you get caught. Lifting the sheet reveals her mangled body.

Road accident.

Pronounced dead on the scene.

Catastrophic head injury.

All these things are detailed in her file.

I glance down at her missing arm.

"Shit!"

I reach over her cold and crushed body, frantically searching for her other arm, thankfully it's where it should be and I lift it for inspection. The hand's still attached, unblemished, a good specimen indeed. The nails are already painted black as if she's been gift wrapped for me. I move around the table and pull a trolley littered with medical equipment closer. The overhead lights shine off the scalpels, needles, stainless bowls and myriad of saws.

I pick up the bone saw and heft it in my hand, acclimatising myself with its weight.

I observe the shiny, metallic teeth which are hungry to purchase flesh and bone.

Pinning her cold arm to the metal slab I smile at the nail varnish adorning her fingers before I begin cutting.

ALL THE LITTLE CHILDREN

Maureen lets out a tired breath.

She's completely shattered. She's also let herself go over the last six months, although I'd never tell her that to her face, I prefer my balls exactly where they are thank you very much. Her hair has become a greasy bird's nest that sits atop her gaunt head. *When did she get so thin?* I wonder as I take in her skull which now dips in slightly at the temples. The skin that covers her skull a pallid jaundice yellow, eyes sunken and ringed by dark patches of skin like a racoon.

She's knackered, barely keeping it together. She shuffles her skeletal frame to the edge of the sofa, pauses. The thing she's been working on so diligently since getting home from her shift at the hospital is cradled in her lap. As she stands she hugs the diabolical creation to her chest, the *thing* she'd sworn me to secrecy over hangs lifelessly from her arms.

"They wouldn't understand," she'd said, and to be honest I don't understand it either.

SHE'S ALWAYS worried I'd flap my gums and expose her.

"If work finds out what I'm doing they won't be very happy. I'd lose my job, or maybe worse. You won't tell anyone will you Derek?" Concern had raised her voice an octave, but still she sat flaying another of those little, lifeless bodies.

I said I wouldn't, not that I speak to anyone anyway. Thinking about the words I might use to explain her actions just felt wrong. I'd never want to speak her horrors into being, I'd keep my mouth shut, for now. God knew she needed help.

The thing she doesn't seem to understand is that if her work did find out about her little side project, these things; they wouldn't be clapping her bravery in the face of Covid, quite the opposite they'd be turning up in a white van to section her and carry her kicking and screaming in a straitjacket all the way to the loony bin.

As SHE HOLDS that thing to her chest I have to remind myself it's not the first, as if somehow that statement makes it bearable, but by God I pray it'll be the last.

I can't stand it anymore.

THE LOOK in her eyes when I'd mentioned she needed to stop, that maybe she'd done enough damage already, was chilling. Somehow the woman I'd known and loved for thirty years wasn't present in that moment because a stranger stood before me; dressed in the flesh that previously housed my wife and best friend.

'*What big teeth you have grandma?*'

Maureen had changed somewhere along the way; and now she was nothing more than a monster.

I remember a dream I had after one of our many confrontation. I woke, in my dream; to find her standing at the foot of the bed, a kitchen knife clutched within her hand and one of *those things* balancing and jiggling on her hip as she bounced it up and down motherly. It hung there all lifeless and limp; limbs flipping about like broken, useless appendages. She was shouting at me about how she loved them too much to give up on them. That if I wasn't with her, I was against her and she'd have to make sure I didn't tell a soul. She approached the bed, knife raised and ready to cut my tongue out. Thinking about it now still makes my blood run cold.

Much like theirs.

THESE LITTLE ATROCITIES she's concocted, fixated over endlessly; poured her blood, sweat and tears into *need* to stop arriving in our house. Whilst she working she has that crazed look of an addict, jaw clenched, skin pallid and clammy. These awful, bastard children are her heroin.

She doesn't realise there's too many of them now. We're quickly running out of room to store their tiny bodies; soon we won't even be able to hide them away when family come to visit. They're literally taking over the house.

I lean back in my chair, place my hands on the greying anti-macassars that cover the arms. Maureen shoots me a cutting glance. I stay put whilst she contemplates going to the front door. It's the same scowling grimace she sends my way each evening of the NHS clap. She's wondering why I'm not getting to my feet, trundling to the door with her, arm around her waist and putting on a united front for our nosey bloody neighbours. I just shrug my shoulders, peer around her at the TV and she eventually leaves me to my woe and utter contempt at what she's become.

"It's for you darling, you're a hero. They appreciate all you're doing during this pandemic!" I say the same thing each time, but inside I'm screaming. *'You monster, when will you stop!'* Her godawful obsession has put a wedge between us which is widening with each new arrival.

She fires a sarcastic smile in my direction, which quivers on her lips like an angry dog, as if the emotion is foreign to her features. I've not seen her smile in years, her attempted smile is quite unsettling. She turns away, taking her smile with her and inwardly I breathe a sigh of relief. Gently she places her latest project onto the sofa and marches to the door to stand on the stoop and watch the street serenade her with clapping.

If only they knew the monster they worship.

She's angry when she comes back, muttering something about slamming the door in their smug faces. Neighbours she tells me, who she'd heard ranting at the NHS not months before this pandemic arrived for taking too long; for not being good enough and being cesspools of germs and infections. Now that the country's faced with an end of days situation, these smug little arseholes give her lip service and adulation. They're terrified of the virus, whilst I'm petrified of the monster they applaud.

"They don't understand!" Maureen rages as she walks across the room, obscuring my view of 'Would I Lie to You'. She sits back down on the sofa and from the corner of my eye I notice her pick up the tiny body and place it on her lap. Her anger quickly turns to gut wrenching sobs as she gently caresses the disjointed limbs in her lap.

"It's okay darling, mummy will make you better," She utters between sobs. I'd comfort her but the work of her hands sickens me, and I'd rather let her stew in her own misery.

She continues to mutter under her breath about the neonatal unit, the small bodies she has to care for and the mothers that grieve with the news their child didn't make it. I've heard it all before, and I'm not going to entertain it. Every time I do, every time I feed this diatribe, she comes home with another one, one time she even brought home twins. With each body that comes through that door she's hoping this time she'll be able to make it work. So I keep quiet and dip a Hobnob into my cup of tea.

When I pull the biscuit out of my tea it wobbles, reminding me of those limbs that dangle from the torso of that thing Maureen's desperately trying to fix. I can't eat it now and so I let the biscuit drop into the cup before placing it on the table and attempt to ignore the frantic movements of my wife's hands.

Maureen tuts, lifts one of the tiny arms up before it flops down uselessly at the side of the baby. She grips it tighter, her hand swallowing the arm like a tiny twig before she snaps it off. The limb tears away from the body and sounds like Velcro being torn apart. She dumps the limb on the floor; a leg soon follows, wrenched from its socket and flung away to join the other discarded limb. It's at the mercy of her powerful hands; the baby's head leans towards the side of its vacated limbs. She turns it reverently, taking in her handiwork.

She slams the body down on the cushion in her lap before she begins prodding at its stomach. Her fingers dig into the torso before she pulls a pair of scissors from her cardigan pocket. She contemplates her incision point briefly before plunging the open blade into its belly button where she begins sawing and snipping towards its neck. My stomach rolls as I feel the acrid tang of bile rising as I know what comes next.

With the incision made in a ghastly Y formation, her dextrous fingers reach inside, ripping out its innards which spool over her lap and fall to the floor in ribbons.

I glance away briefly, but I'm eventually drawn back to the carnage. I can't help but watch her work. However heinous it is, I can't deny that there is also some beauty to it too, however macabre it may seem to the untrained and uninformed eye.

The body's splayed out on her lap, all hollow and empty. Deflated is the best word I can think of to describe the horror staining my eyes.

Reaching to the basket by her side, I notice some of the baby's innards caught around her wedding ring.

From the basket she removes a tiny leg. Inspects it by holding it up to the light. She seems happy with her choice, and places it on the cushion. Her hand dives back into the basket again, this time she pulls out an arm. Holding it between her hands she bends it at the elbow, testing its durability. When she's happy with the movement of the joint she places it next to the hollowed out body, a knowing rictus wriggles across her face.

I turn the TV to another channel and 'The Chase' is about to start, it's a repeat but I've not seen this one.

When I glance back Maureen's started to attach the limbs. She's using black thread to stitch the baby back together. It looks ghastly with the thick black threads connecting new limbs which don't quite match to the peach coloured body.

A Frankenstein child.

A mismatched and hideously crafted abomination.

Once done she places the needle between her thin lips. Her work's almost complete, another child will soon be added to our growing family.

She pulls a bag closer. This one has all the innards she'll ever need, the offal of the previously eviscerated children. She thrusts her fingers inside, grips a handful of the guts and pulls them from within in a never ending stream.

She begins stuffing the child. It's the most peculiar of things seeing a child inflate.

With each handful she stuffs inside, the body rises as if she were breathing air into its lungs, but she's not; she's just ramming more and more innards in, with no care or attention to where they'll end up. Her hands are covered in soft guts, more spill out from the baby and cover the cushion. There always appears to be too much, but Maureen will stuff it all in. I'm always taken aback at how much she's able to cram inside these tiny children.

A few prods later and the stomach is rounded and plump. She holds up her new creation and its eyes are open, blue and hooded. The limbs dangle freely as she inspects her work. Placing it down she commences with sewing up the Y on its torso, frantically forcing the needle in and then yanking it back out.

She pauses.

"I almost forgot, how silly of me!"

Reaching her bony fingers inside another bag she pulls out a velvet heart. She kisses it before placing it inside the chest cavity.

"There you go my little cherub." She mutters, before pinching the wound closed and finishing off her needlework.

Each time she creates it takes so much out of her. She cuddles the child to her chest as the television continues in the background.

She's fast asleep when the contestants lose and I grow bored and turn the television off. Maureen's snoring fills the room as I stand and creep towards sleeping mother and child, before gently plucking the baby from her grasp. I hate holding these children, but I cradle it in my arms nevertheless and walk from the room, away from the scene of the crime.

I enter the hallway and notice the door to the study is open a crack, inside is inky blackness which conceals its residents. I generally keep the lights off in there so I don't have to see the horrors it contains when walking past, but with each new arrival I'm forced to turn the lights on and face the hideousness that resides within.

I push the door open and turn the light on and all our special children stare back at me. Their crocheted bodies sit on the shelves, knitted faces all frozen in place as their sewn eyes watch my every movement. Each of them houses a velvet heart that will never beat, entombed in chests that will never know the warmth of life.

With each hideous rendering Maureen creates, she's always trying to mimic our darling daughter, but they'll never match her beauty. My eyes glass over with tears, as the pain of grief washes over me again.

Each time I'm faced with these lifeless children the wound our daughter left in my soul tears wide open.

I stride into the room and place Maureen's new creation on the shelf with the others.

When I walk away I swear I hear one of them giggle behind me.

I don't look back although I desperately want to, I just turn the light off and close the door behind me, locking them all inside.

CUCKOO, CUCKOO, CUCKOO

I wake in the dark with a foul-tasting rag in my mouth.

I try to lift my hands to remove it, but something restricts my movements. My wrists are bound to a chair. I attempt to move my legs but they're fastened tight too.

In my struggling to free myself I discover water sloshing around my ankles.

Then I remember.

The hand that reached around from the backseat of my car. The cloth which was held over my mouth and nose, and the sweet-smelling aroma that followed; then nothing but utter darkness.

Something moves behind me in the dark; a slow tack-tack of heels on concrete step closer. I peer over my shoulder but it's as dark as pitch back there.

I want to scream.

I want to ask what I'm doing here, but the gag that's lodged deep makes that an impossibility. It's stuffed so far in my mouth that I'm afraid any attempt at conversation or guttural expression might leave me choking on my own words.

Something soft touches my arm.

In the darkness it feels like a tongue snaking its way across my exposed skin. I flinch, the water in the bucket sloshes and splashes up my calves.

A hand grasps a tuft of my hair, yanking my head back. I still can't see my aggressor; sight doesn't seem to work here, wherever here is. With my neck exposed as if waiting for someone to open a new airway I feel their breath on my face; warm and wet, their panting. The smell of strawberries and cigarettes lingers on their breath. My head is suddenly flung forwards, as if whomever holds me captive is disgusted at what they've caught.

Someone's standing in front of me, I can't see them but I can hear them breathing; and I note the gravel on the floor crunching under their indecisive feet. They're waiting, biding their time. I struggle within my binds again as the chair creaks in protest against my feeble attempts at escape.

They laugh.

The cackle sends a shockwave through the room that hits me like a slap and I flinch backwards.

The laughter stops suddenly. The only sound that remains is the slopping of water in the bucket where my feet are and the groaning wood of the chair as I relax back into its clutches.

"Cuckoo!" The sound's sharp and high pitched. It reverberates around the darkened room and I can't help but visualise an abandoned warehouse.

The sound's not from an antiquated clock but spoken by a person.

"Cuckoo..." they're on my left now.

"Cuckoo..." my right.

"Cuckoo... cuckoo... CUCKOO!"

The voice screams into my face but the darkness continues to conceal my aggressor. Their sweet but foul smelling breath pours from their mouth and dances across my face.

I attempt to force the fabric cork from my mouth with my tongue but it's useless. Opening my jaws wider, I feel the duct tape pull at my skin, they've done an impressive job and imprisoning my screams. I swing my head forward like a wrecking ball, hoping it will connect with a face, break teeth or crush a nose; but there's no resistance, I hit nothing but air.

A deep and thoughtful exhalation emerges from the darkness and I'm able to pinpoint their position, they're standing right in front of me; watching my struggle, just out of reach. I lift my head and peer into the inky blackness and align my eyes with where I assume their face to be.

"Only when we've lost everything, are we able to find something to cling to..." the raspy voice utters, unmistakably female; a Northern Irish lilt to her words.

"And you're desperately clinging to hope it would seem." I hear the tack-tack of her high heels again as she totters back and forth in front of me.

I struggle again in my binds, feel them loosen ever so slightly around my wrists.

"It's pointless, you know. You won't get out of here; alive that is. Do you remember how you watched *him* struggle?"

"What are you talking about? Who?" I want to scream, but the gag keeps the words at bay. I try to listen to my surroundings, attempt to ignore the clacking of her heels as if she were a giant insect with chattering mandibles waiting patiently in the dark to devour me when the time comes.

I hear traffic, the slosh of cars on a wet road. Had it been raining when I got in my car? There's wind howling from an open or broken window. The sound of distant laughter and revelry, a pub maybe? Then underneath it all, the far off sound of a juddering train.

But closer, within this room; is the unmistakeable sound of squeaking rats.

As I think about where we could possibly be she strikes me in the face. My head whips to the side and I instantly feel the prickly sting of an open wound as blood begins to slick my face. I note the sound my blood makes as it drips onto my trousers, similar to the tapping of rain on a canvas tent.

"You took everything from me. The nest I'd rendered all these years is now redundant. The baby I'd grown within me, nurtured into a young boy... gone in an instant. You don't remember do you?"

The fresh cut on my face weeps more blood onto my trousers, a damp puddle forming in my crotch.

"Your face was the last thing he ever saw in this sorry world. This stinking place where people like you get away with the things you do; well not any longer..."

Her heels click away, then I hear her returning dragging something heavy across the concrete floor, grunting all through her exertions; her struggles subside once she's in front of me. She disappears again before returning with something that sounds like a skipping rope being dragged across a playground.

I still can't place the woman, or the boy she grieves?

She begins fussing with the assembled items.

Bright, white sparks suddenly light up the room as she rubs what appear to be two metal clips together. The sparks spay into the gloom, dancing briefly in the air, they alight on my flesh before winking out of existence.

The room is once again bathed in all-consuming darkness.

"You were drunk and young. You hit him with your car."

The recollection lands with all the force of a guillotine.

I'd buried it so long ago I'd somehow forgotten it ever happened. Bile begins to burn its way up my oesophagus as the repressed memories grow arms and reach down into my gut, dredging it of its contents, sifting through my foulness in the hope it'll find some shred of guilt or memory of the boy I'd forgotten all about.

I retch in my seat and the chair clatters against the ground as I choke on the rising vomit. With no way for it to escape my mouth it eventually burns its way out of my nose in a hot acrid mess. I'm forced to gulp most of the lumpy stomach-stew back down, as I fight the possibility of choking to death.

Finally, I swallow my shame; a tainted last meal.

"Ah, you remember. Do you also remember getting out of your car, seeing him lying on the roadside, his limbs twisted and contorted; the side of his head scooped out and splashed across the road? You do, don't you?"

My breathing becomes ragged, I'm hyperventilating. The miasma of bile lingers on each harried breath.

"I couldn't see my boy at the end. The coroner said I should remember him as he was and not what he'd become, not what you'd turned him into."

The sparks light up the room again as she scrapes the metal clips together. I make out red and black plastic handles with coppery teeth protruding from each clip. They're jump starter cables.

"Why did you leave him to die alone?" She begins to sob uncontrollably, every now and then the cables touch and errant sparks bloom like fireworks in a midnight sky.

"Cuckoo!"

The noise rings out again. It's the eeriest of sounds now I know it comes from her.

"CUCKOO! FUCKING CUCKOO!" She screams, flecks of spittle land on my face, her temper and quest for vengeance escalating with each passing moment and savage recollection.

"That's what I've called you all these years. For thirty-four years I've called you Cuckoo. I had to give you a name, I had to call you something, I needed to vilify the man that took my boy and Cuckoo served its purpose. That's what you are, a Cuckoo; like the bird. You stole into my nest and destroyed my life, our life. You ripped it apart when you killed my little chic... my little boy... you left him on the side of the road to die like a lame dog. People saw you there before you drove off. You fled the scene leaving destruction in your wake, a mess for someone else to clean up."

"But you'd stopped! You'd gotten out of your car, I just can't understand why you didn't help my boy? I don't even want to hear why you did what you did, that's why you're fucking gagged; nothing you say, no reason you could ever give would ever excuse you for what you did. I don't need to hear your lies or your begging. You're a murderer, and I've had a great many years to plan your penance."

I want to tell her I'm sorry, that I didn't know what I'd done. At the time I was quite possibly drunk; I couldn't go to prison, I had my whole life ahead of me. I can't recall the day or the boy clearly, but if it happened like she said it did; he must have been dead when I got out the car?

I want to tell her that now, that her son was dead and I couldn't have done anything about it. But was he? The whole things a blur, a memory belongs to someone else. I know she's going to kill me, and isn't that what I deserve?

Karma's a bitch.

"You were the last thing my boy ever saw, so it's only fitting that my face should be the last thing you ever see..."

The woman sparks the wires again, this time near her face. She appears from the darkness like a Caravaggio painting, chiaroscuro in fluid motion, her features made only of light and dark. She's old and hunched. Her boney arms hold the cables taut, her wrinkly flesh is liver-spotted and papery thin. Grey hair hangs limply around her face as her weathered face leers up at me.

It's her eyes that haunt me most. Although they're illuminated by the sparking lights they're completely lifeless. Dull-grey orbs like worn pennies, scuffed by time, circumstance and years of heartache. They're devoid of love, as if they only observe pain and suffering now.

Her eyes are also shielded with cataracts. Any forgiveness or pity she might have offered me are forever stuck behind those tainted lenses she sees the world through; growing spoiled and more clouded with each passing day, like a glass of milk left in the sun.

As I stare into her soulless eyes, I realise that there's no hope for me.

She plops one of the cables into the water.

My heart begins to hammer in my chest.

"Goodbye, Cuckoo!"

She drops the other cable in the bucket also and the electricity burns through my body; white and bright and incredibly hot. My jaw clenches andI hear the enamel of my teeth pop and crack against each other; limbs spasm uncontrollably within their binds. My skin feels as if its being flayed.

Smoke rises as I witness the flesh of my chest bubble and blister; the skin splits open, allowing fluids to sluice from within. I stare out of eyes that won't close and through the smoke that billows around me I see the boy standing before me.

The side of his head's missing and a rictus grin stretches across what remains of his bloodied face; his mouth opening and closing like a fish as he hobbles forwards. His last words if that's what they are become lost for a moment in the chaos.

His words find me now as I give in to the pain.

Three words I refused to hear after I got out of the car.

His final plea I refused to answer.

"Please... help me?"

The boy shuffles forwards, his words repeating over and over.

I can't look away from the horror I made of him with my car.

My guts give way as my chest blooms with fire. The flames that engulf my face and strip my skull of flesh also steal my final breaths. I finally stop struggling and surrender myself for the eternal punishment that awaits me.

A PLACE TO LAY
ME DOWN

H enry Harper sat at the bottom of a grave; a broken shovel
at his feet.

He was cursing his luck, and the loss of his trusted
friend and tool of the trade. The grave was deep in shadow, the
sun not high enough in the sky to warm his skin. He stood now in the
depths of the soil and bemoaned his loss.

"Damn infernal contraption." He spat before kicking the shovel.

Henry turned from his fallen and trusted friend. They'd buried so
many people over the years and now, in a way, it was his turn to say
goodbye to his companion. He just wasn't ready to say it yet.

Down in a vacant grave was where Henry felt most at home,
where he belonged. Grave digging was a lonely existence, but he
didn't mind; he had no family or friends left, because he'd dug their
graves too.

He wiped the sweat from his brow, reached out his hands and
gripped the rickety wooden ladder that leaned against the side of the
grave. In that moment he realised how utterly alone he was, and
smiled at the thought, taking solace in the fact that he'd outlived
many of the town who'd strived for the finer things in life.

'*What'd that get you?*' he thought, a chuckle leaving his throat. '*A seven by four hole, is what it gets you.*'

Climbing the rungs of the ladder, he left the darkened depths behind as he emerged into the world he felt he didn't belong but must always return.

Once out of the grave, he walked its perimeter. The sun was warm on his face but not yet high enough to heat the cold pit below. Pausing he bent down and picked up his drink. It was empty. Henry cursed the day.

When he'd woken this morning he knew it was going to be pig shit, and here he was with a broken shovel, no refreshment and he still couldn't figure out his damned crossword puzzle.

Crushing the can before he threw it into the darkness.

"Damn you all the way to hell!"

Suddenly a murder of crows exploded into the sky like a black firework, all feathers and flight. Henry reached into his front pocket, removed a pen and tucked it in a well-practiced routine behind his ear. Returning to the same pocket he removed his bifocals and put them on. Turning with a heavy heart he headed toward his van which was parked on the access road. As he wandered through the many graves, a testament to time and his dutiful work, he pulled the crossword puzzle from his back pocket.

"Reticent; set aside – eight letters?" he muttered aloud, to the many ears of the dead.

Passing two well-kept graves he paused, turned to one of them and smiled in recognition.

"What do you think my love?" He asked the marbled stone. Moss had begun to climb over the lettering. Reaching forwards he picked some off, revealing the name.

Elizabeth Harper

"What's that love?" Craning his ear toward the grave of his late wife, "It's not like you to not have an opinion on the matter, cat got your tongue?" He began to chuckle, but his laughter died in his throat when to his left he noticed his son's grave, much smaller, with a waterlogged teddy bear tied to a three foot cross as if it had been crucified.

"Sorry my love, just having a pig-shit morning. This damn crossword has me rattled but I'll get there, I always do. Well I best be off, gotta get me a new shovel and a drink. But I'll be back. I'll come back to tuck you both in when it's dark." Henry shambled away.

He'd buried the both of them, too. Other men had said they'd take care of the formalities but he wasn't a slacker by any sense of the word and who better to intern his family for all of time than the man who'd cared for them their entire abbreviated lives.

He fell into the drivers seat of his van, crossword still in hand. He held the crumpled paper in front of him before smoothing it out over the steering wheel. The puzzle was pretty much completed, he just needed one last word before he'd be able to draw a line under it and place it in the drawer with all the other ones. He knew the word ended in a D – but that left a whole seven other letters that he just couldn't place. Throwing the crossword on the passenger seat, he turned the key in the ignition and drove into town.

HE PARKED the van in front of the library across from the hardware store where he'd pick up a new best friend. One that was made of wood and metal, a dear friend that wouldn't talk; but listen as they worked the soil together. He preferred his friends like that – silent; because when he was eight feet below the surface he'd hear things... voices. '*Groans of the grave*' he called it.

Down below he felt he could hear the many buried voices conversing through the mud, silt and loam. But he never told anyone; they'd think him crazy, they'd ask him not to come back – and he needed this job. He was good at it, and the voices liked his company. They told him secrets they hadn't uttered in life, yet in the finality of death, their tongues were loosened and they spilled their guts.

"Reticent; set aside – eight damn letters." Henry grumbled as he reclaimed the crossword and stuffed the paper into his front shirt pocket before exiting the van and heading to the hardware store.

"Hey!" a voice suddenly split the stillness of the morning.

Henry checked both ways, desperate to ignore the shrilly voice. Just as he was about to step into the road, a hand gripped his shoulder and spun him around.

"Hey, I'm talking to you Henry!" It was Derrick, the librarian, a fucking busybody if ever there was one.

"Hi Del, what's chewing your ass out this morning?"

"Nothing. I've been hollering, didn't you hear me? Anyway, you can't park your van there. Can't you read?" Derrick pointed to a sign hanging on a traffic cone behind him, "Says 'Reserved'... I've got a delivery of books coming soon and I need to unload it and your van's in the way. You'll need to move it. Now."

"Del, I'm only going to be a few, I gotta pick up a new shovel and a quick drink."

"Move it. I won't be telling you again."

"I ain't moving shit, you want it moved, you move it."

"Look Henry, just move the damn van, what's the rush? The dead'll wait for you, they ain't going anywhere." Derrick pointed at the sign again as if to further his argument. He'd always been a stickler for the rules since school, where he was bullied for being a mummy's boy. Henry knew Derrick's pedantic nature made him the perfect choice for the librarian job, always telling people to be quiet, always wanting to silence everyone. He never wielded that power at school, but now, the bullied became the bully.

"The sign says reserved. Move your fucking van or I'll get it towed."

A crowd converged and people began to stare, they were muttering about 'Crazy Henry' their voices were loud and their looks long.

"I'll be just a few, like I said. You want it moved you move it," Henry leaned forward, his voice pinched to a whisper; "You get it towed – just remember I know where you live, mummy's boy, and I've got a plot of land that's begging to have your name etched in marble. But I'm done talking, you do what you do, and I'll deal with the consequences."

Henry turned and walked away. The rubberneckers that had converged began to disperse, they'd all been hoping for a scene, a punch thrown and claret on the ground. Across the road now, Henry could just make out Derrick cussing him to the stragglers in the crowd before the doors of the hardware store closed behind him. Blessed silence reigned once more.

PLACING his new best friend next to his chair in the coffee shop, Henry ordered a latte to go, because graves don't dig themselves and time was money. A grave digger has one job Henry mused; *to dig the grave before its eternal resident shows up* – and he didn't want to keep them waiting any longer than needed. He held the crossword out before him, mud from the morning's digging was trapped under his nails. Henry scanned the letters in the boxes and ruminated over the clue.

"Excuse me sir." A young girl's voice pulled him from his cross-word conundrum. *This better be damn good* he mused.

"Yes dear?" He said to the tall drink of water; a pretty little thing, hair in bunches with a figure-hugging uniform. She smiled and all the prettiness vacated her face as Henry took in the braces across her teeth which caused her mouth to pucker like a cat's anus. *Must be a summer job* he thought. *I'll go easy on her.*

Noticing the young girl shift from foot to foot, he could tell she was visibly uncomfortable about the task at hand.

"You can't sit here I'm afraid."

"Sorry dear, what now?"

"My manager," she hefted a thumb over her shoulder. Henry

observed a stern-looking elderly lady glaring from the counter. "She sent me over to tell you that you can't sit here. It's *reserved* for a function and well, they've paid for these tables." The waitress moved her finger around as if drawing an imaginary circle with him at its centre.

Henry sat there, quietly judging the waitress and the manager; he reached forward and picked up his shovel, the metal head scraping on the floor. The young waitress back-peddled, fear etched across her face – He wondered if she thought there was going to be a moment. Standing he hefted the shovel in his hands before pointing the business end at the elderly manager.

"I'll move, I was just resting my bones you old bint. If you'd be so kind as to bring me my bloody drink I'll be on my way. *Reserved.* What a crock of shit, that's all I been hearing today – can't a man just go about his day without being harassed?"

The mousy waitress retreated before returning with his latte in a take-away cup, placing it on the table. Henry rummaged in his pocket before depositing some change into the girls shaking hand.

"For your trouble. Don't go giving that hag any of it, you hear me, it's yours, you earn't it!" With his shovel in one hand and coffee in the other, he peered intently at the manager, keeping her in his gaze as he walked around the table and to the door.

"With any luck you old crone, we'll see you soon," he uttered before lifting the shovel and brandishing it at the manager, indicating the '*we*' of his slur. "I've got a plot with your name on it." With that final remark, he left the coffee shop and trotted to his van.

Climbing inside the van he noticed Derrick struggling to unload the delivery that had been forced to park further down the street. He smiled before chuckling to himself as he watched Derrick struggle with the boxes of books. As he pulled out of the parking space, Henry beeped his horn and gave Derrick a wave. Derrick returned his gesture with the middle finger.

He was about to stop the car and bludgeon Derrick with his new friend but he kept on driving, he had bigger fish to fry today. Finishing the grave and figuring out the damnable crossword were his top priorities, but he didn't fret, he knew he'd get there in the end. Usually the voices of the dead helped him when he got stuck, all he had to do was dig a little harder and deeper and listen for their groans.

HENRY DID some backbreaking work once he got back from town. The grave was deep enough to bury several people. The tip of the ladder barely touched the top of the grave. The soil which was piled high along one side, again ensured the sun would not shine down on him today.

Henry sat on the third rung of the ladder and mopped his brow. He thirsted for another drink but he'd run out again, so instead of a liquid refreshment he sat in the coolness of the shadows with his crossword in hand.

"Reticent; set aside – what the hell are you?" He uttered, pulling the pen from behind his ear and tapping the paper impatiently.

Just then, a groan came from his right. He peered at the dirt, the mud all carved smooth by his dutiful digging. The groan came again, which was quickly followed by another. Henry stood, shuffled closer and crouched near the wall. Placing his hand against the cold earth, he brought his ear closer to the wall and waited.

He desperately wanted to hear it again because it sounded like a word.

"Reticent." He whispered.

Mud fell from above, landing on him like dirty rain. Glancing up he was expectant to see someone staring down at him, the person wondering why he was at the bottom of a grave and doing a cross-word of all things; but there was nothing but blue sky. Henry felt the wall throb under his palm, as if the mud was breathing. Instinctively he pulled his hand away.

"You're trying to tell me aren't you?"

A long groan as if someone were stretching sounded around him;

as if his interned audience were trying to converse with him, desperately wanting to utter the word he longed to hear.

"Do you know what it could be? Reticent; set aside? Eight letters? Ends in a D." He watched on as part of the wall crumbled away. He'd had graves collapse on him before, but this was different. He realised the crumbling was nothing to do with the complexities of grave digging but caused by something trying to burrow its way through the soil and into the open grave.

Frozen to the spot as if his feet had grown roots, Henry peered at a hole appearing in the mud. He leant forward, focusing intently into the widening gap. He felt air coming from within, *but that's impossible* he thought. He quickly assured himself it was the summer breeze tumbling and swirling down from the graveside.

Then he heard it, the small voice calling out from within the hole.

"I'd be damned." He uttered as he shifted closer. Indeed, he could hear a muttering coming from within.

With his ear to the hole he felt and heard the subtle exhalation of a held breath. Then, a word. Or, part of a word.

"*Res...*" the raspy voice uttered.

"What was that? Is that the word? For the crossword? I knew you wouldn't let me down, speak a little louder... I can't quite here you."

His head was flush with the cold mud now.

The voice came again, loud and clear. It was the word that would complete his crossword and seal his fate.

"RESERVED!" The voice screamed from the hole.

Henry stumbled away and tripped over the foot of the ladder. Scrambling backwards he peered up at the hole where greying fingers were wriggling their way through the mud like worms. Soon the digits began tearing away clods of dirt from the sides of the grave wall, as if whomever was on the other side was frantically trying to get to him.

He was about to scream when a set of children's arms burst through the mud beside his head. Their cold and dirty hands sealed his mouth closed, trapping his screams within. He thrashed his head frantically, trying desperately to loosen their hold. Soon more hands reached out and began to secure his legs. Other clawing hands emerged from the bottom of the grave and secured him to the ground. More rotten limbs burst from the walls around him and as the mud crumbled from the walls around him it revealed many leering faces with mouths full of blackened, gnashing teeth.

Some screamed as they pulled themselves free, mud tumbling from their gaping maws.

They wasted no time in welcoming Henry home, at last.

As the grave collapsed in on itself, Henry's last thoughts were of his wife and child. He mumbled his last words though a multitude of dead fingers and loam, and it sounded to the murder of crows who perched in a nearby tree as if he'd said, "Together at last."

Henry, hadn't made this reservation, but he'd be keeping it.

HAIL MAUD FULL OF GRACE

Maud had lost herself again in fervent prayer.

She was slouched behind the wheel of her 1964 Pontiac Bonneville. The car had once been a bright powder blue, now it was covered with a patina of rust that gave it the reddish-hue of an old scab.

Her head rolled to the side and her eyes grew wide as she strained to see where she'd ended up this time. The lights from outside were like stars dancing across her vision. She noted that darkness had begun to take hold of the day, its unstoppable black hands wringing the very last rays of light from the sky like the remains of breath from a throat.

Maud's vision finally cleared and her eyes focused on the liquor store that appeared outside her window. She winced at the harsh glare of the neon blue *Bud Light* sign that hung in the window; she was outside ***Howie's Wines and Spirits***.

The familiar sinking feeling washed over her like the onrushing tide. Soon she'd be lost beneath the current again, giving in to its relentless pull and the incessant calling of the deep; whether she wanted to go or not.

Peeling her eyes away from the sign, the haunting recollection it birthed lessened its grip on her mind.

She knew why she was here – now – because she did the same pilgrimage each year; an appointment she had to keep, like a barn swallow returning to its old nest.

Maud noticed a police cruiser parked in front of her Bonneville, the officer strangely absent.

Probably inside buying donuts or booze, it's all they're good for, the filthy pigs.

She wondered if the officer might have pulled her over for dangerous driving?

Is that why I was praying, did I kill someone?

The thoughts assaulted her like a hoodlum from the shadows and she grew even more agitated, her fingers tapping out the beats of her racing heart on her leg.

In her sudden dread Maud looked around frantically for signs of life, half expecting to see a child in the road; an innocent bystander she'd mowed down after falling asleep at the wheel.

In her panic her eyes fell on a picture of her husband, Elmer; hanging from her rear-view mirror.

"Oh Elmer, how long has it been my dear?" She uttered into the quiet of the car, her thudding heart calming just at the sight of her beloved. His smile was a soothing balm to all her worries, and apparently in the moment an antidote for her panic.

Shifting her gaze from her husband, Maud took in her own reflection and stared at the haunted eyes that looked back from the mirror.

Wrinkles creased her once smooth brow, and crow's feet now accentuated the corners of her baggy eyes. Maud let out an exasperated breath at the sight. Raising a hand she swept a clump of grey hair aside; as she tucked the strands behind her ear, she paused midway through her action. Her eyes grew wide and her jaw slackened, the sight of blood sickened her.

Pulling her hand down she stared at the ichor gracing her knuckles. A deep, maroon crescent was carved into her flesh.

How on earth?

Maud reached into her pocket, pulled out a handkerchief and began dabbing at the tacky blood.

As she applied pressure to the wound, trying to stem the flow; she peered out the window at the liquor store. Since she'd been taking blood thinners, she bled like a bitch from even the most innocuous of abrasions.

As she continued to stare out the window she noticed that the streetlight outside the store was still out. The darkness afforded by its absence was thick and ominous, and only the cool, blue light from the Coors sign announced the few people coming and going from the store.

"They've still not fixed that light Elmer. They said they'd fix it, damned liars!" Anger tampering with her voice.

She pulled the handkerchief away and tucked the bloodied fabric back into her pocket. She watched her knuckle closely as the blood bloomed once again in a small bead of red, where it rolled down her hand like a tainted tear until it slowed before trickling down to her wrist.

She needed to leave this place, get away from the memories, flee the scene of the crime of long ago. She desperately needed to get back to the land of the living and not succumb once again to preserving a ghost. Maud shot one last glance at the liquor store, her eyes finding the single candle shining in the darkness. It was situated near the automatic door; accompanied by a single rose and a picture of Elmer in a glass frame, the same picture hanging in her car.

Tears began to crest; she used her good hand to wipe them before reaching for the keys. She checked her wing mirror and noticed a tyre iron and a scattering of bolts on the ground outside. She paused.

"That's odd, why on earth–"

The answer to her befuddlement came from her wounded hand as it ached afresh. *Maybe that's how I cut my knuckle?* She'd never been good at these things; that had been Elmer's department. Her predicament became clear; the police cruiser had stopped to help.

Maud sat in the car unsure of what to do, her thoughts still racing away from her. *Why do I keep coming back to the spot you were murdered?* The darkness didn't answer. The anger and injustice of the affair burned through Maud in that moment and it wore her down, her eyes stuttering closed like a set of broken blinds. But she wouldn't sleep; she'd pray, and so she placed her head on the head-rest, tears streamed down her face.

"Those bastard pigs need to pay!" She muttered before she began praying.

"Hail Mary full of grace..."

MAUD WAS PULLED from her prayer with a start; someone was tapping on the window. A flashlight shone through the glass and she had to squint to see past the beam. She quickly peered in the rear-view and noticed another cruiser had pulled up behind her; she was sandwiched between the law now, and there appeared no way out. Another impatient tap on the glass followed and Maud grabbed at the handle and wound it down.

"Good evening, catching a nap were we? Licence and registration,"

"Is something the matter, officer?" Maud offered as she reached to the glovebox. From the corner of her eye, she caught the officer moving his free hand to his gun. *Always so eager to shoot someone,* she mused.

"No problem ma'am, I just saw you sitting here, this isn't the best part of town for someone to get some shut eye, especially a woman and if you don't mind me saying, someone of your age. It's an *accident* waiting to happen is all."

Accident.

Maud winced at the officers choice of words.

"You should be on your way."

"I wasn't sleeping officer, I was praying."

Maud reclined into her seat and passed the licence and registration. The officer shined his flashlight on her hands as he snatched the documents, and she pulled her hands back quickly but the flashlight followed them into her lap. Maud covered the cut with her other hand.

"You're bleeding ma'am." He said before redirected the beam to her documents.

"Oh, yes. I was trying to change the tyre and the tyre iron slipped... When you get old officer, your skin turns to paper, the slightest thing can cut you wide open. I'm just happy that the other officer," Maud pointed to the cruiser in front of her. "Arrived when he did, a real hero that one."

The policeman passed Maud's documents back and Maud placed them on the passenger seat.

"What time was that ma'am? When the officer stopped to help you?"

"Oh," Maud glanced at the clock on the dash "I'd say it was about an hour ago?"

"Right and you've seen him since?"

"Yes, officer. He was standing where you were, asked if I'd like him to help get me back on the road." The policeman shined the light on the cruiser in front, then to the tyre and tools spread out on the road behind.

"Is there a problem officer?"

"You say you've seen him in the last hour?"

"Yes officer, he was here, well, he was here before I started praying, such a polite young man, Pete Stanhowzer."

"Sorry ma'am you know Pete? Officer Stanhowzer?"

"Yes. Of course. I know you too, Jimmy Cole." Maud watched as the officer furrowed his brow at the mention of his name.

"I made a point of learning all your names, you were so helpful when my husband was murdered right over there. That's his shrine." Maud nodded to the candle guttering in the breeze.

"Your husband?"

"Elmer Kemper."

"But you're..." The rest of the sentence lodged in the officers throat.

"White? Yes, I am – how very observant officer."

At the mention of her husband's name and the officer's racial misjudgement, his face flushed red. He lifted a hand to loosen his collar as if a noose had suddenly tightened around his neck. Jimmy was flustered by the unpleasant recollection.

"You've still not fixed that light." Maud retorted as if it were the cop's job. Jimmy glanced over at the dark shadow engulfing the store's entrance. His eyes lingered and Maud imagined what he might be thinking.

"It's okay Jimmy. It was reported as an accidental shooting, wrong place, wrong time. It's been fifteen years. I just come here on the night of his passing to light a candle. There's something poetic about that don't you think? Each year I come back to keep his memory burning. I've aged, and I don't blame you for not recognising me, but you and Pete haven't aged a day. I'd recognise you two anywhere!"

"I'm... I..." Jimmy stuttered as Maud quietly assessed him. Her words seeming to sever his vocal cords.

"You were the first responders weren't you?" Maud offered, as she glanced once more in her mirror. Jimmy just nodded, shifting his weight awkwardly. *He's begging for the ground to open up and swallow him whole,* she mused.

"You were called out to a robbery, a black man had apparently held up the store. That's why you shot him wasn't it?"

"I'm sorry for your loss. It was a tragic accident, we..."

"Yes. Yes. Terrible wasn't it. The shooting of an unarmed black man, an innocent one too. Most of them are though, aren't they? It seems all they're ever armed with is skin that attracts police bullets like metal filings to a magnet." She shook her head.

"My dear Elmer had popped out to get me a pack of cigarettes and while he was there, he picked up a bottle of wine. I do like a tipple in the evenings officer, but I've not had a drop tonight; I can assure you of that. I believe that bottle was the cause of all this turmoil, the root of this so called '*accident*' as you put it so deftly in your reports."

"It was dark ma'am, we couldn't see him. The streetlight was out. The light from the sign, it shone off the bottle, it looked like a knife... We told him to stop, to put the knife down. He never said it was a bottle. We'd never have..."

"Opened fire? But you did! You saw what you wanted to; a black man with a weapon and opened fire, again and again." Jimmy's face crumbled and he placed his hand on the door, pain and shame eating him alive.

"It's okay Jimmy." Maud placed her hand on top of his. She felt him flinch, but he didn't pull away. "You were just doing your job, but you pigs just can't shoot black people and ask questions later. Can't you see the countless black lives falling like dominos?"

Jimmy pulled his hand away after her use of the word 'Pig'.

"Ma'am you said you'd seen officer Stanhowzer, where is he now?"

"He's in the store. Said he needed to use the little boy's room. He was doing such a good job with my tyre before that."

Maud watched Jimmy fiddle with the radio clipped to his shirt pocket, nothing but static came back. He then shined his flashlight over to the liquor store, searching for the missing officer.

"Jimmy." Maud uttered sweetly, and he turned back to her.

"You wouldn't mind helping a frail old woman by finishing what Pete had started would you? I'd do it myself but..." Maud held up her bleeding hand, feigning inability.

"Of course," Jimmy replied, more out of guilt than anything else.

Maud couldn't help but think Jimmy would do anything in that moment to erase the way he'd murdered her husband.

"You stay right there and I'll get you on your way."

Maud wound the window up and watched Jimmy work. The car rocked as he went to work on removing the flat. She glanced up at the photo of Elmer.

"It'll be over soon darling. I'll put all this to rest soon enough."

Maud clutched the steering wheel, her knuckles bone white, the strain she put on the leather splitting the wound on her knuckles open again. She watched the blood trickle from the gash and drip onto the wheel. The pain made her feel alive. Watching it drip her prayers began to fill the car one final time.

"Hail Mary full of grace..."

ANOTHER TAP on the window and Maud turned her head, her prayers cut off in an instant. She wound the window down and let the cold night air spill in.

"All done Mrs. Kemper, if you'll pop the trunk I'll stow the flat for you."

"Oh it's a bit fiddly back there. I'll come and help." Maud pulled the keys from the ignition.

"No need ma'am, it's the least I can do."

"No I insist," Maud opened the door and stepped out.

"Why don't you give me that," Maud gestured to the tyre iron in Jimmy's hand, and he quickly surrendered it.

"I'll carry that and you can bring the tyre, I'm sure a big strapping man like yourself could manage that." Jimmy nodded and did as suggested.

Maud shuffled to the back of the car swinging the iron like a metronome. Peering over her shoulder she noticed Jimmy bending down to pick up the flat before she cast her eyes to Elmer's candle, it was still flickering in the wind.

The street was deserted, not a soul about. *Good,* Maud thought as she placed the key in the trunk and turned it. The lock surrendered but the trunk remained closed.

"It's open, but my hand hurts like hell warmed up. You wouldn't mind would you?"

"I've got it. Let's get this stowed and have you on your way."

Jimmy gripped the handle to the trunk as Maud stepped closer, raising the iron.

The trunk opened with a rusted whine and Jimmy peered in. Maud anticipated his hand moving towards his gun. She was on him in an instant, the iron fell through the air like a guillotine, connecting with the back of Jimmy's head. His body fell forwards and came to rest on Officer Stanhowzer.

Maud dropped the iron and set about scooping Jimmy's legs into the trunk where he'd join the other fallen officer.

It was hard work but she managed to tuck him in. She heard a groan, a guttural, nonsensical jumble of vowels soon followed and she dipped low to reclaim the iron from the gutter. Once in hand, she leered into the trunk of horrors. She brought her face inches from Jimmy's crushed skull.

"Shhhhsshhh... there's no point struggling. I knew I'd find the weak link in your cover-up story sooner or later. It's taken me fifteen long years. I've read so many reports, other *accidents* involving inno-cent black men being gunned down on your watch. It was hard to pin down exactly who was responsible, you or your partner. To think of all the pigs I've slaughtered over that span of time, none of which hold a candle to you."

"I knew one of you would talk. One of you would beg and plead. I bet you didn't think it'd be your partner who fingered you as the one who eagerly pulled the trigger that night. He gave you up thinking the axe would forgive, that he'd be spared, but the axe is very unfor-giving and always falls."

Maud lifted her gaze and looked once more to Elmer's candle. It flickered one final time before it was snuffed out.

"It's over Elmer."

Maud took inventory of the contents of the trunk and the twisted, bloodied bodies of the officers that had caused her so much pain. She'd done what she needed to do, she'd gotten closure.

Jimmy's lips quivered, his eyes rolled to the top of his head, a strangulated groan filled the trunk. Maud pondered if that's what Elmer sounded like as he bled out, as these two men concocted the lies they would need to tell.

Maud didn't linger. Instead, deciding that the axe of justice wasn't finished, she lifted the tyre iron and let it find its mark again and again and again.

MORTAL WOUND

The cedar tree where we first kissed stands before me. I don't know why I've come here, for all it houses are memories I'd do best to forget.

Its limbs spread heavenward, layer upon layer, the perfect visual expression of a family tree. Wider at the bottom where we'd belong, I glance up as it grows taller and thinner, reaching to the blue sky where our ancient ancestors sit in the heavens at the top looking down with scorn and judgement.

The sun's out and a light sweat dampens my underarms as a trickle of moisture snakes its way down my back. My blouse sticks to my flesh in all the wrong places. It's claustrophobic and feels as if clammy hands are smothering me, which is an odd sensation given the open fields that abound. It's in this moment that my thoughts turn to you and the cruel work of your hands on my flesh.

I observe each layer of the tree as I approach, each adding to the next in a canopy of interconnectedness and I realise that's why I've come; to feel closer to you. Even though you're gone I can't escape your presence as it appears in life all around me.

Even in death your little atrocities remain.

I shuffle under the sagging green limbs that hang low, worn down by time, but perhaps it's the memories of us being here that wilt its branches, the roots soaking up our past failures. I know first-hand how oppressive the weight of defeat can be. It's taken a long time to stand straight and hold my head high, but I'm getting used to this new view.

Within this space I feel safe, it's as though the branches reach down to embrace me, to hold me close and protect me. As the wind moves through them I hear the tree sigh, as if it feels sorrow for me. As if this testament to patience and time, of growth and renewal has witnessed my sluggish withering under your hampering shade.

I press forward; walk to the trunk that bears us witness. Etched deep within its bark remains our declaration of love, a scar on the world.

I press my fingers to the wound, the tips of my fingers trace the darkened etching.

TC and JP 4ever

The memories hurt and so I glance away. I stand at the foot of the tree and stare into the canopy above. I'm struck by the warmth of the sun that dapples my flesh, as if being kissed for the first time.

With my fingers still tracing, I realise that in a strange way I am part of something bigger; overwhelmed by this titan of the forest, the one we marred with our ignorance.

It hasn't succumbed to the wound but it does show that to persevere is to flourish and through it all we can survive.

I suppose that's what I am really, a survivor.

You see, the rings inside a tree denote the passage of time and circumstance. I have my own internal rings, aged bruises and broken bones covered by new layers of growth, which mark the passing of my own life, my own circumstances; but you can't see them for looking at me because my flesh is now free of you.

I turn, place my back against the tree and slide to the ground. The bark announcing itself as it scratches my skin through my top. It's nice to feel something other than your fists or the fear that clung to me like a second skin. I sit, my mind returning to all the times we came here, to our tree.

The Seventh Kiss

We were once said to be *young love's dream*, until things turned sour. Before words could wound and strip me of my dignity; they were a poison with no antidote and caused me to lose sight of who I was and what I could be.

You'd clipped my wings.

Your words raped me, cutting deep and true. They compromised my supports and chipped away at my foundations until I couldn't stand straight without your scaffolding. If you'd left, I'd have fallen apart, crumbling to dust in your absence.

When you hear the same thing, again and again you start to believe it, however much a lie you know it to be. To you I was no good, a busybody, a prick tease – a slut; I was an unfit mother, a lay-about, a bitch and as you so eloquently phrased it, a fat pig.

There was no *me* anymore, only *us*. To remove myself from you was a death sentence.

"Who would have you?" you'd said.

I quit my job, my friends, and my family. You bought me drab clothes to stop better men from discovering me. You decided when I could drink and eat and how much and at what time; you also cut my rations when you told me I'd gotten fat. I let you into my head and you ruined me over time, you made me believe I deserved that ruin.

Today's kiss was different from the others, there's a first time for everything I guess. Today you didn't kiss me with your mouth but decided to kissed me with the sharp bones of your knuckles.

I choked on the ground after you'd winded me, then you kissed me again with the toe of your boot. Again and again you showered me with kisses, reminding me how much you cared. But not once did you kiss me with your lips. Our declaration of love presided over it all on the trunk behind you; a taunting whisper from the past.

The Fifth Kiss

This time you truly meant it; you kissed me lovingly with tears slicking our faces. You'd told me it wasn't my fault and I believed you. That passionate kiss was what kept me hanging on, and I hoped that you'd actually changed.

A week before this kiss I'd fallen in the street. I was grocery shopping which was one of the only times you'd allow me out alone. I'd tripped, the bags split and their contents scattered. Fruit and vegetables, tins of food and bottles of beer rolled down the street and into the gutter. I'd gone down hard, hit my stomach on the unyielding pavement. Little did I know then that the pavement didn't hit nearly as hard as you.

I was helped to my feet by an elderly man. As his hands touched my flesh I felt the warmth of a caring embrace and it felt electric. Whenever you touched me it was always cold and devoid of love.

The man helped me to my feet and inspected my wounds.

He bent down and began collecting my shopping from the ground, every inch the perfect gentleman. As he turned back to me the man froze. He was still crouched but was staring at me strangely. He wasn't looking at my face, but lower; much lower than any gentleman should.

It was then I became aware of something trickling warmly from between my legs. Suddenly I realised the life I was carrying, the son who might grow up to be just like his daddy, was leaving this world prematurely. God please forgive me; in that moment, I felt relieved.

I was comforted knowing our son wouldn't grow up under your tyranny, that you wouldn't be able to bend him as easily as you'd bent me. I cried with abandon, but the tears that ran down my face were tears of unbridled joy.

The Third Kiss

This was the kiss you gave the day your hands found my flesh for the first time. Purple welts ringed my neck, the marks of hungry fingers which wanted to squeeze the life out of me. They almost had until you realised what you were doing.

If I'm honest I knew that the beast you hid so well would return because the disguise you wore would only last for so long. How long would it be until you truly hurt me?

You claimed it was *my* inability to give you the child you so desperately craved, that lead to your infidelity. And the thing is, I believed you. Maybe my womb was a hostile place to raise a child; my fear of bringing another *you* into this world polluting the very soil in which our baby would grow.

I should have left then, I should have got out whilst I still could, but you pleaded with me to stay after you removed your hands from my throat. The fear in your eyes at your transgression was convincing enough to make me stay.

Your embrace felt like a bear trap and I your wounded prey. I knew that if I struggled to break free I'd be injured and you'd find me as I limped away, you'd track me down and kill me. So I stayed.

The Second Kiss

This was the most sorrow filled kiss of the lot. It's the one I still have nightmares about, because I chose to stay and fight; but what I didn't know at the time was in choosing to stay I'd already given up any semblance of the fight I had left.

You said you were sorry for fucking that woman, and I believed you. I forgave you.

Promises poured from your mouth like a soothing balm, an anaesthetic to my flesh and resolve. I should have run, I should have fled but you begged me to stay. In my youth and naivety I thought I could change you, make you a better man; but what I didn't know

66

then is that your words were snake venom. Slow acting poison that destroyed me from within, tenderised my flesh and killed my hope. I can see clearly now what you were then, you were my personal Judas who'd betray me kiss after kiss; and I'd allow it, giving you permission to destroy me from that day on. How foolish I was to stay.

The First Kiss Under The Cedar Tree

I gave myself to you wholly as we carved our declaration of love into the cedar tree. I watched on enraptured as the slivers of bark fell to the ground as our promise to one another were etched into the place we called ours.

I'd heard all about your reputation, but I loved you. Those warnings were just words and opinions; I knew *you*, the others did not. I also revelled with the thrill of disappointing my parents; it was their anger at our communion that finally thrusted me into your waiting arms.

You were my poisoned fruit and I wanted to savour every bit of you.

You promised me your never-ending love and life to its fullest. You pledged yourself to me with words of affirmation and thoughtful gifts and of course, that first sweet kiss.

Our first kiss under the cedar tree sealed my love for you but it also sealed my fate.

As I RISE from the ground, my thoughts of you tumble away.

I can stand now. I can move without your shadow looming over me because I became a phoenix overnight. I rose from the ashes of my previous life, I shed the skin of the beaten and oppressed, and picked myself up off the kitchen floor.

I emerged from my battered and bruised husk a changed being that had decided I would no longer be marred by your hands, belittled by your words or owned by your tyrannical rule. I would no longer flinch when you came close, cower when you shouted or flee in fear. I would never again cry when you forced yourself upon me.

I can do all this because I decided to thrust the knife; again and again. I hacked and slashed, severing the ties that bound me to you, each swipe liberating, each slice enabling hope to bloom from the wounds I inflicted on you.

I'd stared down at your corpse a survivor.

As my final goodbye, I make sure to proudly stick the knife I'd used to cut you from my life into that ugly scar we inflicted on that tree all those years ago when we were young loves dream.

TRAPPED IN THE AMBER
OF THIS MOMENT

Her flesh. Sapling fresh, bruises at will.

I shouldn't but I couldn't...

Hands grope, devour her throat, corrupt her flesh one last time. Bedaub her once radiant skin with my unrelenting love for her.

I shouldn't but I couldn't...

Gnarled tree root fingers find purchase, a windpipe. She grows cold, my hands hot. Searing her flesh. They brand her with my touch. Stain her one last time — in the most beautifully tragic of ways.

I shouldn't but I couldn't...

I hold her down within the crashing waves, secluded amongst the rocks, hidden from the revellers on the beach. Foaming waters muffle her half-hearted whimpers of submission, her eyes fearful. Knowing. I hold her there, screams buried deep within the slag heap of noise — hiding our secret, our pact.

I shouldn't but I couldn't...

A crack sounds within her fleshy prison of a neck. Head lolls to the side. Struggles end. I let go. She's at peace. Suspended in the ebbing tide, back and forth. Glassy eyed and pale skinned – if the sea were amber she'd be my mosquito forever.

I shouldn't but I couldn't...

'If I get cancer, the terminal kind. I want you to end it for me,' she'd said. 'Cancer will not have this victory.'

I shouldn't but I did...

CASUALTIES OF WAR

The man standing at the checkout in front of Eric was bleeding.

His arm was missing, blood spurted from the gory hole in his shoulder, a socket as white as snow gleamed from the raw meat where his appendage should have been.

Eric mused that the geyser of claret that sprayed everywhere was possibly from a torn artery. He was no medic but had seen his fair share of torn and dismembered bodies; enough carnage to last a lifetime and then some.

Claymore, RPG's and IED's could all be the culprits. No matter the design of the bomb, devastation and dismemberment soon followed, and since Eric had been back home, these visions showed up at frequent intervals.

He'd seen these horrors of flesh before but that didn't make it any more palatable.

Eric noted that the man was bleeding all over his goods and the tide of blood was ebbing its way closer to Eric's bottle of whisky and packet of mints.

This man wasn't the first Eric he'd seen and it wouldn't be the last. They had a way of finding him when he least expected, but recently they'd been showing up with more frequency, as if the dam that housed them had broken and there was nothing to keep them at bay.

Eric had left much of himself in Afghanistan during his two tours, and he'd brought more than he'd ever bargained for back with him to the real world; and the horrors just wouldn't relinquish their grip on him.

They were persistent like cancer, never ceasing or never giving up their torment of him. However much Eric begged them to leave, however often he screamed himself awake, they remained, steadfast. They'd never let him forget the horrors he'd been party to.

Eric stared at his bottle of Bells and the packet of extra strong mints on the conveyor belt before checking his watch. He still had time to get himself right before his meeting. The drink helped to keep him steady and operational, and sometimes it even helped to dull his waking nightmares.

Everyone had their way of coping; many of his platoon found theirs at the sharp end of a needle or the business end of a gun, but Eric's way of surviving came in a glass bottle and a screaming hang-over. He could live with that, it was just a shame his wife couldn't.

Eric's wife left him not long after he returned from his final tour. He'd choked the life out of her one night when she tried to wake him, but all Eric saw was a corpse reaching out, the skull blackened by whatever blast had torn the poor bastards face asunder. He'd felt the phantom's throat crunch as he bared down with all his strength, desperately trying to stop their grabbing hands.

His wife packed her bags that night and fled whilst Eric sat in the shower, letting the water wash away his resolve, shame, sins and the memory of his nightly visitor.

When he finally went to get help, the doctor said he was suffering from PTSD.

"Hey mister, you wanna shuffle down some?" It was the cashier.

Eric glanced up and noticed her smiling face.

He peered at her name badge, Melissa. She had two stars next to her name, there had been a third but it looked as though one had been removed somehow. Eric shuffled forward and glanced down at the floor, he expected to see blood, but all he saw was as a squashed grape and an old receipt.

Moving past the cashier he began rummaging in his pockets for his card.

Melissa held the bottle of whiskey aloft and called for someone named Bob to remove the anti-theft device around its neck.

"How'd you lose the star?" Eric offered, the cashier just stared at him, chewing her gum.

"What was that?" She replied, a look of confusion wrinkling her young brow.

"The star." Eric pointed at her badge. "You're missing one?"

Eric glanced down at the card in his hand, he was shaking; not because of the woman serving him made him feel nervous but because of the visions he desperately needed to drown before their ugly heads rose above water.

When he glanced up Bob had been and gone, and was halfway back to his station. Eric watched on as the man scratched his arse before heaving his rotund frame up onto his chair, where he sat like a sniper in a bell tower watching over the checkouts.

"Bob did it," the girl said.

Eric turned back to the girl as she continued chewing her gum, mouth opening wide with each chew of her cud. The wet sound her mouth made was reminiscent of fingers picking through torn flesh in search of a bullet.

"What now?" Eric said as the girl slid the bottle of Bells toward the bagging area.

"Bob, that sack of shit over there," Melissa gestured in Bob's direction. "He took a star off me for chewing gum at work, but I ain't gunna listen to him. He's just pushing his weight around, God knows he's got enough to spare. He just wants to get in my pants."

"Oh right." Eric said, trying to steer the conversation away from the girl's underwear. *Had she dropped that on purpose? Was she flirting?* It had been so long since he'd played that game he no longer understood the terrain anymore.

"How much do I owe you?" Eric uttered as he picked up the bottle and pocketed his mints.

"£11.33, you paying by tap or chip and pin?"

"Chip and pin?" Eric phrased his response as a question, unsure of what the correct answer should be.

"Alright old man... just warming it up for you." The way she'd phrased those words made Eric think of prostitutes and dirty old men.

"Old man?" Eric said peering intently at the girl, gauging her response. She was right; he was probably old enough to be her father but he wasn't an 'old man' by any sense of the word.

"Yeah. Chip and pin... my parents use that. I'm just saying it's pretty old fashioned; like the Rolling Stones, come to think of it, which stone have you been hiding under? I've never seen you in here before."

"I'm just passing through." Eric kept it short and sweet.

"Okay, cool, but times change man. You can just tap that shit and go." She lifted her fingers and grabbed at the gum in her mouth, twisting it around a dainty finger. Eric mused that her customer service skills needed some work. The Army would have chewed her up and spat her back out like that piece of gum she was so intent on twiddling, they'd have beaten her into shape. But he liked her spunk and the total lack of respect she held for the establishment she worked for.

She was punk and he admired her for that.

"It's ready now grandad," Mellissa said with a laugh as she sucked the chewing gum back off her finger.

Eric tapped in his pin and waited for the confirmation, half expecting to see Bob march over and strip another star from her badge, a public dressing down, court-martialling her where she sat.

"You can take your card now," Melissa said as she turned away and began to scan the next customers items.

Eric removed his card, lifted his gaze to say thank you and that's precisely when he noticed the back of Melissa's head missing. A large exit wound sat in the middle of her blonde hair, fragments of her skull poked out like a crown made of bone. Blood dribbled down the back of her uniform, puddling beneath her on the leather seat. The back of the chair was covered in an assortment of greyish meat, the splattered remains of her brain.

Eric turned quickly, he didn't want to see the ruin that awaited him if she turned and gave him a flirtatious wink goodbye.

Before reaching the exit he'd already uncapped the bottle and taken his first calming chug of many; there was still time to drown the ghosts before his meeting.

ERIC WALKED TO HIS MEETING, making good time; at this rate he'd be able to sit in the park and finish his bottle before having to check in. The sun beat down as he struggled through the hordes of people going about their days.

He stopped outside a butcher's to remove his jacket, once freed he noticed the rings of sweat under his arms; which transported him back to the desert and the gear he'd had to wear. He breathed a sigh of relief and relaxed in the knowledge that it was only a memory.

"You couldn't spare any change could you sir?" A weak voice pulled Eric away from his sweaty pits. Glancing up he noticed an old man sitting on an upturned milk crate, one of his legs was missing. Eric waited for the blood, and the disembodied leg to appear in a gory puddle at his feet; but his eyes alighted on the hand written sign the old man held in his lap.

A veteran of Desert Storm, injured in battle, homeless and hungry. Eric weaved his way through the people passing the fallen hero like he was a piece of rubbish, completely unaware that it was people like him that had fought for the peacetimes this generation squandered so freely.

Eric dipped his hand into his pocket and removed a few coins. It wasn't much but it was something to show he cared for the man's plight. He dropped them into the old boy's tin cup, Army issued and riddled with rust.

As the coins hit the tin they rang out like hostile gunfire; each percussive noise made him flinch as they boomed loudly around him. Eric closed his eyes as the last coin fell, but it didn't ring out like the others, instead it made a wet slap.

Opening his eyes Eric saw the tin can was laying on its side, the money spilled out across the street. Near the coins he noticed a trail of blood smeared across the pavement which lead to someone's gore-riddled jaw bone. A wheezing began to emanate from the veteran, and as Eric turned he discovered a cavernous, red hole where the man's mouth had been moments before.

The veteran began to talk, a flaccid organ that Eric assumed was his tongue danced out of his mouth freely like a wet whip. Unintelligible words filled the air as the veteran struggled to replace the slick jaw bone, desperately trying to shove it back in place as blood drooled from his mouth in a never-ending tide of vermillion.

Eric stumbled back and was buffeted by the crowds. People cussed him as he tried to get away from the grisly scene playing out before him. There was a break in the crowd and suddenly Eric discovered man was nowhere to be seen; another ghost, another soul, another dead body that had decided to follow him home.

Eric, backed against the butcher's window, thankful to have something solid behind him. Reaching into his jacket pocket he pulled out the bottle, his liquid comfort and bastion of courage. Unscrewing the lid he took a large hit, looking ever more the drunk the people passing by thought he was.

As the guttural assertions from the war hero played over and over in his mind, Eric took another gulp before screwing the lid back on.

With his desperation sated he leaned back, the glass of the shop window cool on his scalp.

Suddenly a loud bang shook the glass and he snapped back to attention. Spinning around he expected to see a red-faced shop-keeper shooing a day drinker away, but all Eric saw was a leg hanging in the window, suspended by sharp silver hook. The ball of the femur poked out from the combat trousers like a marbleised cauliflower. There were also rips in the fabric and pieces of mangled flesh were visible within. A dark liquid ran from the bottom of the trouser leg, flowing over the boot like treacle; dribbling a dark gruel over the sausages and chops which were warming in the shop window.

Eric looked closer, rubbed his eyes to see if the vision would leave, but it didn't. The detached leg involuntarily twitched again, a spasm of severed nerves causing the boot to kick the glass over and over. Eric fled before the glass shattered and the limb came hopping after him. He spent the rest of his walk on tenterhooks.

Along the way he passed a lady who was screaming at a man about him grabbing her arse, but in Eric's mind it was and angry mother holding a dead child out to a soldier, demanding justice for what they'd done to her child. Eric took a deep sip from his bottle.

A group of teenagers hurled stones at an abandoned building, the sound of popping glass was reminiscent of gunfire and Eric scuttled for the safety of a doorway. Peering around the corner he attempted to locate the sniper from his cover, but there wasn't a sniper, there never was. He took another long draw on the bottle before leaving and wondered if he was losing his mind.

He kicked a discarded beer can and it rattled along the pavement, the liquid that remained inside aided its continued rotations. As it turned, again and again; it morphed from beer can to grenade to beer can, a never-ending torment that caused Eric to run.

HE WAS three buildings away from where the meeting would take place and slowed from a sprint to a gentle amble. His shirt was soaked with sweat and stuck to his back. His chest looked as if he'd taken a bullet, a damp, dark patch spreading across his front.

Spying the park across the road he lifted the bottle to the sun; a quarter of the bottle remained. He decided he'd finish it in the park and then head back to the meeting, a little late but he needed the liquid courage right now, as the visions were gaining strength.

Sitting on a park bench he watched as people moved around him, oblivious to his inner torment. They stared at him and he also noticed mothers pulling their children away as they passed. Eric assumed they were casting aspersions about his sorry life, imagined them discussing what had driven this haunted man to drink a bottle of whiskey at eleven in the morning; but he didn't care. He was a bum, a train wreck of a human; tormented and close to breaking.

'Screw them and their opinions'

Eric noticed a girl out of the corner of his eye. He wouldn't usually have paid her any mind, but she was a blur of furious motion; running with a purpose, desperation in her stride and a steadfast look of hate all over her face.

He followed her trajectory, she was running towards a group of school children who were all busily talking, completely unaware of her approach. The park soon faded away and the girl was now running across sand; the buildings around them riddled with bullet holes, it was a war zone.

Eric glanced back at the group of children, but they were now civilians, villagers, women and children. He felt his pulse rising, his heart racing; he wanted to shout but his mouth was a desert, his voice a dried-up thing in the back of his throat.

Then he saw the cable and the way it snaked from her hand and disappeared into her backpack, her thumb poised over the detonator.

He began shouting, but his voice never left his throat.

As the girl made it to the group she stared back at him, a rictus smile etched into her angelic face as she pressed the detonator.

The shockwave of the blast made Eric's legs go weak and he collapsed onto the park bench. His head pounded, bright white flashes ripping through his brain, bleeding into his vision.

Finally, there was silence.

No chattering, no talking, no birds singing, no car engines, no screams; there was absolute nothingness, and the nothingness was deafening.

Eric opened his eyes.

The sand was gone, the emerald grass before him was littered with body parts, a huge crater sat where the children had been chatting. Arms and legs were strewn across the ground, guts hung from tree branches; burnt bags and blackened belongings were littered around the blast radius.

Eric stared at the ground a few yards in front of him, his eyes drawn to the only movement in the desolation. Smoke drifted like early morning mist, and from within came fingers; fingers attached to a hand that was attached to an arm. The arm stopped just above the elbow, the skin a tattered trailing mess like the tentacles of an octopus.

The fingers moved spider-like across the ground as they hauled the remains of the arm in its wake, leaving a red smear behind it like a slug trail. It skittered closer, closing the distance rapidly before Eric kicked the arm onto the grass where it frantically righted itself to resume its attack.

As it skittered closer Eric charged forwards and stamped on the appendage, crushing the fingers to a bloody pulp before jumping up and down screaming into the war-torn park.

"Hey!" The sudden interruption shocked Eric from his crazed stamping.

A man stood before him, protectively shielding his child, and Eric saw the frightened, tear-streaked face of the little girl peering out from behind the man.

"I think it's best you get on your way before I call the police, there's families here man. They don't want to be seeing some drunk losing his sh... cool in front of everyone, so have some respect. Where's your dignity?"

Eric wanted to say his dignity was lost somewhere on foreign soil, buried deep with the blood of the innocent he'd slaughtered; rotting in some hellscape with the body parts of his friends. But he didn't.

Eric drank in the fear on the little girl's face before he noticed her father's balled fists, his knuckles bleached white with the duty to protect all he held dear. Eric uncapped the bottle and finished it off in front of them.

"Sorry, I'm sorry!" He mumbled as he turned away, staggering up the path to throw the bottle into the bin.

As he shambled up the path he heard the little girl speak.

"What's wrong with the bad man daddy?" Her voice an angelic song.

"He's not bad darling, he's just dealing with something we know nothing about. So do you want the swings or the roundabout?"

"Roundabout, daddy!"

Eric turned to see the two trotting over the grass towards the playground, oblivious to the battle field they were traipsing over, of the landmines and tripwires en route or the corpses they were disturbing as they fled from the bad man.

Eric approached the steps to the meeting and took the packet of mints from his pocket before quickly stuffing three into his mouth at once. He chewed them immediately, the sound rattling his head and reminding him of tactical boots on the ground, soldiers marching into battle.

Eric surmised it was always best to arrive not stinking of booze, because if he did, they'd ask questions and there was nothing he hated more than questions. He decided to slide in unnoticed, grab a coffee to mask his breath and in an hour he'd be out. He'd go home with another bottle or two inside him and hopefully he'd have drowned the visions by then and he'd get some much-needed sleep; oh god, how he needed sleep.

As he stepped into the room he scanned it for threats; a habit that never leaves a soldier that's seen combat. The need to check for exits, threats, dead zones and kill corridors was forever ingrained.

All that was visible to Eric after his brief search was the circle of people sitting on foldout chairs in the middle of a dimly lit room. There were a few empty chairs so Eric grabbed his coffee and shuffled on over. He wanted to sit as far away from Jennifer as possible; she ran the PTSD group and had a nose like a fucking bloodhound. She'd smell the drink for sure, so Eric made a beeline for a chair opposite her, across the circle.

The group had already begun and Jane was retelling her recurring nightmare. She was trapped inside a burning Humvee as the fire cooked her alive. Apparently in that moment, when all was lost, she'd found Jesus. He'd been sitting there with her the whole time she'd said; keeping her safe and alive – she said it was like that story about Shadrach, Meshach and Abednego from the bible, something about the fiery furnace.

Erik thought her delusional, but there was something about her face, a look which certified the truth in her words.

She turned to the group with her hands held together as if in prayer and offered them salvation if they were brave enough to ask for it. Eric glanced around and knew from the looks on her audiences faces that most of them were scared shitless of this higher power she spoke of. They were cowards who relied on the draw of a bottle or the depress of a syringe to fight the fears that stalked them all, it didn't make them addicts though, in Eric's eyes it made them survivors.

Jane stared at Eric and he could have sworn he heard her skin crackle from across the room as the charred remains of her face failed to display the smile she was desperately trying to show the room.

Suddenly there was movement behind Jane which drew Eric's attention; ghostlike figures stalked the perimeter of their circle, he knew no one else saw them, they were his burden and his alone.

The ghosts always encroached when his guard was down, and they'd congregate in baying masses of leering faces. They shifted, mouths snapping out of the darkness, gaunt and bloodied atrocities, all casualties of Eric's war.

He knew they were more than that however, they were his private hell, his conclave of retribution, and they would make him pay for his war crimes.

His eyes darted from face to ghostly face. Each a villager he'd tried to subdue. They had greying eyes and screaming mouths, forever frozen in cries for mercy. Darkened, wet holes glistened in the centre of their heads. The very spot he'd placed his gun that sealed their eternal silence.

The one behind him placed her hands on his shoulders, her cold breath tickled his ear as she bent down to whisper to him. She begged him in broken English to spare the lives of her children, her mother, and her village.

She was the only one that ever spoke, his personal tormentor; the one that would walk him all the way to the grave and what waited for him beyond.

"Eric?" A sharp voice cut off the whispering of the dead woman.

Eric glanced up from the greyish fingers holding him down. He realised quickly that if he kept his eyes on Jennifer he could almost ignore the dead souls prowling behind her.

"Sorry?" Eric offered.

"Are you okay? You seem miles away." For a moment Eric couldn't help but think she was trying to sniff him out, giving her a reason to grab him after the session and bend his ear about being good to himself.

"I'm fine, just a bad night sleep is all."

"Right, well do you have anything to share with the group this week?"

"Nope. I'm actually coping pretty well at the moment, adjusting to the new medication and keeping busy. Nothing new to report." He smiled at Jennifer and sat back, took a sip of the foul-tasting coffee before he felt the tugging hands of a thousand souls reaching out from the grave to claim him as one of their own.

As they pulled at him, picking over what remained of his stinking soul, the ghosts sifted through the butchery stored in his mind. They dug deep, discovered the murderous acts of war he'd justified by his lies. They worked the edges of his untruths before tearing his mind to pieces, revealing what he'd buried all those years ago.

The ghost behind him had seen enough.

The woman whispered something Eric's commanding officer had told him after a particularly productive and bloody day.

"The first casualty of war is always truth!"

Heads That Could Shatter Glass

The baby was screaming in the back seat, a bewailing that would have the devil scurrying from its wrath. The boy's face was slick with tears and snot dribbled off his chin in translucent cables. His appearance had morphed from peach to red and now the deep purple of asphyxiation.

Brad sat in the driver's seat, hands pressed hard against his ears trying to drown out the never-ending screams. He was stopped at a red light, which seemed to be in cahoots with his son – torturing him – he just wanted to be moving.

When he was moving, Jacob would relax, his eyes would roll in their sockets and his little head would almost instantaneously grow too heavy for his tiny neck. That's why Martha sent him out, to get their son to sleep.

'Drive him around for a bit, get him tired; asleep if possible and then bring him back. I can't take much more, Brad; he's shredding my nerves, if you don't take him I'm going to do something; something I'll regret.'

How could a father refuse? Brad left with Jacob in tow.

There was a good part of town, but they didn't live anywhere near it, and so father and son cruised the streets he'd never be brave enough to walk at night. He'd been driving for twenty minutes when he arrived at the stoplight from hell.

As he checked his surroundings he saw someone lurking in the shadows by the alleyway to his right. A pimp, a prostitute, a dealer – Brad knew it would be some undesirable; you'd have to be desperate to be in this part of town after dark.

Suddenly the figure approached the car and Brad quickly hit the central locking. Peering in through the window the figure appraised what was locked safely inside. keeping his gaze forward, Brad ignored them, maybe they'd just give up and shuffle back into the shadows. Sure enough, the figure skulked by and disappeared back into the shadows to sniff some glue or shoot some dope, leaving Brad to deal with problem #1; his son Jacob and his vocal discord.

He couldn't tell who was worse; the street urchins outside the car or his banshee of a son melting his brain with his incessant screams.

"Shut up, shut up, shut up!" Brad screamed, spittle flying in all directions. His shouting only serving to worsen things, as if this was an involuntary competition and he would lose no matter what.

He was about to get out the car and allow the dregs of the night to help themselves to his son. He placed his hand on the door and pulled the handle gently, but it didn't open; he'd forgotten about the internal locking mechanism. It served just the right amount of time he needed to realise leaving his son to vagrants was not a good idea. Martha might have something to say about that course of action when he returned home minus their son.

Brad looked again in the rear-view mirror and watched his writhing offspring fight with the straps pinning him into his baby seat.

"Come on buddy, give daddy a break yeah!"

Jacob returned fire with both barrels; a sonic assault that almost flayed Brad where he sat.

"Come on you pig-shitting lights, come on!" Brad bashed the steering wheel with his palm, peered around outside once again as if contemplating his next move. The night was deserted apart from the shadows that cluttered the street corners and alleyways. There wasn't a car in sight, the whole of Main Street was devoid of traffic.

"Fuck it!" Brad slammed his foot down and the car lurched forward, the screaming of tyres a blessed relief from the strangely similar squealing of his son. As the rubber protested Brad shot another glance into the rear view and was amazed at what he saw. Jacob had stopped crying – a bloody miracle – *there is a god after all.*

He was flying now; the car was an unleashed beast carving its way down Main Street.

"That's better boy isn't it?" Brad shouted to Jacob who was now watching the show as they passed under the streetlights at high speed, an orange strobe effect dappled the interior of the car. Something fell onto the floor in the back of the car and Brad glanced over his shoulder quickly as the speedometer continued to rise.

Jacob had a dour look on his face and his bottom lip began to quiver. Brad shot a fleeting glance back to the road before returning to locate what had fallen; he needed to act fast, for the volcano that was his son was about to blow its top one more time.

Manoeuvring his arm into the back of the car he found Snuffles – his son's tatty old bunny. If he didn't get the damned thing back in Jacob's chubby little fist soon the moment of peace would be over, and he was pretty sure the next screams would shatter the windshield.

Brad tried and tried again to shove the bunny back into his son's lap but he wasn't taking it; if anything he was kicking it petulantly from his outstretched hand. The car swerved as Brad continued to try and his foot unwittingly pressed down on the accelerator; they were literally flying now.

"Take the damn bunny Jacob!" Brad shouted, thrusting the toy blindly, hoping to feel it pulled from his hand sooner than later. But all that came was a blood-curdling scream.

Peeling his eyes from the road he gave the bunny one final thrust but still Jacob wouldn't take the damned thing.

Suddenly his son stopped screaming.

Brad looked up at Jacob's face and noticed his son's eyes had grown wide. He realised too late that his son wasn't looking at the bunny or him; but was staring past them both at the road ahead and the obstruction that had shambled out from the darkness.

Brad didn't have time to stop. A shrouded figure bounced up onto the hood before its head connected sickeningly with the windshield, spiderwebbing the glass. A gory clot of flesh punctuating the centre of the web on impact. Frenzied, Brad took his foot off the gas and as the car slowed he could hear the grinding of metal. Peering through the fissured windshield he noticed a crumpled shopping cart being dragged alongside the front wheel.

As the car came to a stop the body rolled off the car and landed in the road with a wet thump. Brad sat there, the sound of the body hitting the car playing over and over in his head. He was curious as to why that sound was crystal clear, and then he realised Jacob was finally quiet.

Brad looked around, peering through the shattered glass, uncertain if anyone was out there, and he wasn't about to get out and check. Thoughts tumbled in his mind; *there's a way to get out of this, drive home, ditch the car, escape while you can and still have a life worth living – I've hit a homeless man, who's going to miss him? Surely I'm doing the city a favour?* It was then that Brad heard a sound that changed everything. A slow chuckle crept from the back, then became a jubilant giggle. His son was laughing.

"Again. Again."

Brad shook his head.

"Again Daddy, peas... again!"

Brad put the car in reverse, the cart squealed and buckled as it broke free from the front fender. He put the car in drive and navigated his way around the wreckage in the street. He peered down at the body and where the face of a person should be was nothing but a bloody mask. Brad tore his eyes away from the carnage and drove away from the scene of the crime at a crawl. He scanned the road checking to see if anyone had seen him but the place was deserted; they were safe, for now.

As they cruised well under the speed limit Jacob started up again.

"Fast... daddy, gain... gain... GAIN!!"

Brad winced at the shrill voice that peeled his brain apart and watched in disbelief as Jacob began screaming and gesticulating to the windshield, at the gory bullseye, dead centre, blood trickling down and bleeding across the fractures.

"No!" Brad shouted into the din.

"YES!"

"No. We're going home, and you're going to bed!"

"Poop!"

"What did you say?"

"Poopy Daddy!"

Brad turned left onto Chapel Road which would lead them home, back to Martha and Jacob's bed. As they approached another set of lights, Brad slowed; trying to time his arrival and drive straight through once it turned green. Somehow Jacob noticed his slowing and began screaming, grunting his displeasure to his disobedient father; the shrill noise ripping into Brad's head. It was the worst pain he'd ever felt, a migraine of epic proportions, white spots began to bloom in his vision like fireworks in the night sky.

"Stop it!" He screamed at his son.

"Daddy's a bum face."

"No more, we're going home!"

The sounds from his son's mouth seemed to rattle the car. Brad could have sworn he heard the fractured glass crack further and the metal of the roof buckle under the unrelenting pitch.

"GAAAAAIN!"

Jacob was furious and Brad couldn't take anymore, planting his foot firmly on the accelerator. The car lurched and the screaming subsided. Brad noticed his son's eyes in the mirror, they were almost unrecognisable; they were the eyes of a stranger, lusting for more carnage. They quickly passed under the red light and the car continued to build speed; they were a hurtling bullet, hellbent on finding flesh.

"Better Daddy. Bang Daddy. Bang!" Jacob giggled from the backseat.

The bright lights of a nightclub came into view. He saw the mass of people outside, he could see the ropes and the bouncers and knew in that moment what he must do, and Jacob chuckled, a devil on his shoulder.

"Yes Daddy. Bang Bang."

Brad floored the accelerator and the car became a missile hurtling towards the crowd. He only had one thing on his mind. The blessed silence his carnage would bring.

Jacob grew quiet as they swerved across the road, now heading straight for the packed entrance to the club. There would be bloodshed, there would be crumpled bodies and there would be heads that could shatter glass; but there'd be peace that followed.

The car mounted the curb.

Brad looked once more to the rear-view; Jacob had fallen asleep.

Compared to the alternative, the screams that followed impact were music to his ears.

A CAR HONKED and Brad shot awake from his daze, unsure of where he was. His hands quickly danced over his body, checking himself for damage before he turned in his seat to scan the backseat for his son.

Jacob was fast asleep, Snuffles was tucked safely under his arm. Brad looked out the rear window, and noticed a car pulling around him. He watched the car pass, the driver flipping him the middle finger before shouting; "Fucking loser, get off the bloody road!"

As the car drove away, Brad realised he'd drifted off, that fatigue had consumed him at the wheel of his car.

"What a damn dream," he whispered, fearful of waking his son. A moment later he slipped the car into drive and edged forwards, he glanced up one last time to check on his sleeping son.

BANG.

Brad jammed his foot on the brake, his eyes returning to the road.

Standing in front of his car was a homeless man pushing a cart full of cans. Brad held his hand up in apology and the man just stood there staring, shaking his head before lifting his gloved hand and slamming it down on the hood.

That's when Brad heard it, not the metallic thump, but something else, the thing he feared most. It was slow muttering at first, but soon came the full force of the storm. Jacob was screaming again, the same ear-splitting-nerve-shredding screams that Brad had thought he'd silenced.

Brad stared at the homeless man, wondered for a split second if there was any other way to silence his boy, but as he pondered his next move, Jacob turned the volume up to deafening.

Without another thought, Brad hit the accelerator.

CAT BOX

I feel that my whole life's lead up to this moment.

I watch the grainy images of the VHS fill the screen.

An elaborate collection of grisly cutaways flicker strobe-like on the television before the forest appears through a crossfade. It builds until all I can see is a dense forest.

It's quickly followed by a static establishing shot of a big crater full of old junk.

It's Farley Woods, which backs onto our property.

The first time I watched the tape and discovered our close proximity to the legend made me shudder. Knowing that Cat Box existed right on my doorstep, that I was none the wiser to its presence was both chilling and thrilling.

And now I know it's there, it just fills me with an insatiable need to do its bidding.

The VHS flickers between the next set of cuts, as if the tape were about to be consumed by the mechanisms inside. As if the cogs were hungry for the taste of celluloid, but suddenly it rights itself as it always does and the screen blooms with closeups of dead things.

Animal and human by design covered in grisly viscera, poking out from within the dark meat, the bleached white of bone.

Jump cuts soon follow, detailing all of the forgotten things within the pit.

Each piece of rubbish a breadcrumb to Cat Box's location.

China figurines, lamps, beer bottles, dirty bras and used condoms; children's toys and white goods. Everything's bedaubed with rusty smears that could have once been blood, which once resided in a human. The camera pans out to reveal stretched flesh and rubbery innards hanging in trees like forgotten streamers. Blood and twisted entrails, bone and greying organs litter the floor.

Without warning the video stops abruptly. It's a work in progress of sorts, an unfinished piece of art. As if this video is just a prelude, the humble beginnings of what Cat Box will become the more the myth grows.

A blizzard of static covers the screen and white noise hisses through the television speakers like a swarm of angry wasps.

Apart from the visuals there's one thing I've failed to mention. The haunting voiceover that presides over the haphazardly spliced images, the deep, gravelly baritone that intones to whoever watches the film that there needs to be an offering, an atonement of sorts; something to balance the scale and swing the axe away from its chosen target. Me. You. Whoever is watching.

The voice never wavers on the importance of the offering. If anything it gains more power and greater passion with each viewing. Sometimes it sounds as if it's pleading; begging and beseeching its viewer to action.

This wasn't some *Thirteen Reasons Why* bullshit.

There wasn't anything glossy or self-deprecating about this.

This was real.

This was a new gospel to a sick and needy generation.

This was the legend that had been circling the playground and living in depraved minds. The legend of Cat Box.

I believed everything the faceless voice uttered and for good reason too, because each month the school was another student lighter and the lamppost another missing poster heavier.

I for one didn't want to end up on that lamppost like those other tosspots who didn't believe the message they'd received, or the tape that had found its way to them. Their inability to act on the information at hand was quite plainly Darwinism in action.

So there was only one option.

I needed to follow through with what it said, right to the fucking letter.

Cat Box or the person who started this legend obviously knew where I lived because the VHS was waiting for me on the doorstep when I got home from school. No note. Nothing to say where it came from, or who dropped it off. Just the tape inside a tattered slipcase with spidery handwriting scrawled down its spine.

They'd surely come back for me if I didn't do what they said, if I didn't follow through with Cat Box's twisted desires.

Were they watching the house?

Were they waiting to film me make my offering?

Were they going to immortalise my crime on film?

Would I become part of the legend?

Would I become famous?

Over the fortnight I'd had the tape I'd become addicted to its message. When I slept I could see the film playing out on my closed eyelids, projected onto the dust sheet of my mind in all its grainy glory.

I'd committed each depraved image and every sordid word to memory. Each piece of rubbish that lead to Cat Box's location was burned into my mind, they'd become flares and markers for when the time came and I needed to follow the path.

Each syllable of threat spoken by that gravelly voice I greedily consumed until it was tattooed on my brain, where it repeated like an echo in the darkness of my room when sleep evaded me and became just a word.

I'd chant the message in my mind like a mantra.

A blood offering.
Someone you hate.
We know where you live.
We'll kill everyone you love and have you watch.
Find the Cat Box, make the offering, leave the video, be
transformed.
Only in fulfilling your calling and purpose can you shift the
judgement from you.

I eject the tape.

Place it back into the cardboard sleeve.

The title on the label doesn't appear ominous. If anyone found it by accident in their child's room they'd think it was a school assignment or a kid's television show.

But the truth of the matter is Cat Box is a battle cry.

I drop the VHS into my satchel, pull the drawstrings and the opening closes like a noose tightening around a neck. Soon I'll be part of the legend, find myself on that lost footage of the damned and hopefully the judgment will pass from me, where it will find a new troubled soul to torture.

I wonder sometimes how the tape finds its lost souls, or if it's *us* that find *it*.

I pace across the garage and retrieve the bowsaw from the hook on the wall. Its rusted teeth hungry for the carnage that waits to be born.

I turn the lights off and step out into the future that awaits me.

IT HAD all started with the pictures I'd drawn at school.

It wasn't long after mum had left, well fled – that's what she'd said in her letter.

She'd wanted to get away from Dad, he'd been hitting on her, not like adults sometimes do after a few drinks; he'd literally been hitting her, marking her English Rose complexion with fist sized bruises which mottled her skin with yellow, green and rust coloured blemishes.

She hadn't taken me with her, because as her letter detailed she couldn't.

'Your father would track me down, he'd pursue us to the very ends of the earth. He'd kill me for taking his son away from him.
I'm sorry I've left you with him.'

So, I was left alone, with him. Without the punchbag of my mother, I soon became the sack of sand and leather that took the punishment of his fists.

I'd drawn some pictures in my GCSE art class. All of them were graphic depictions of a shadowy, ominous figure that was killing people in abysmal ways. It was always the same figure whatever the medium I decided to use.

Watercolour.

Pencil.

Acrylic.

Clay.

It was always death and blood and the rending of limbs. Life imitating art or art imitating life who the fuck knows and who the fuck cares.

I'd started my journey to Cat Box in those hastily constructed pieces of art, and Cat Box must have heard my calls of despair and the need of vengeance. It was called to my door by my desires to destroy something beautiful. I know this now because not long after I'd drawn those pictures the VHS arrived on my doorstep as if it, or someone was watching my suffering and was giving me a way out.

The portentous figure that I'd drawn was always blurry but the look on my dad's face as we sat at school watching the teacher flick through the assortment of death committed to paper and listening to the teacher ask if everything was alright at home; Dad knew that it was him in those pieces of art staring back at him.

He'd fed the teacher a line about a troubled boy missing his mother, and the teacher retorted some halfhearted response about the school being understanding given the circumstances; that this was a difficult time what with my mother leaving. *Fleeing* I wanted to say but stilled my tongue as my father crushed my hand within his.

The teacher had said that there was of course a transitional period, that young minds deal with trauma in many different ways. But that *'grace period'* she spoke of had long since elapsed and they'd expected me to have somehow moved past all this turmoil by now.

Who puts a timeline of grief?

They'd said that the pictures were a growing concern, and that if something didn't change they'd be forced to conduct some type of investigation.

My dad had leant forward at this point, and as if butter wouldn't melt in his mouth he'd said that it was too many horror films and the imagination of a young boy who'd been abandoned by his mother and that they should cut them some *mother fucking* slack.

Somehow the teacher took the line, out of fear or overstepping the mark I'm not too sure, and we took the subsequent suspension from school, because apparently you can't talk to figures in authority like that, even when you're an adult.

When we got home I took another beating, I couldn't stop him. I was just too small and too skinny to fight back. I was weak and pathetic and Dad was just so bloody strong and relentless. He didn't let up this time, he'd been afforded a grace period of two weeks for the bruises to fade thanks to the school. He went to town with his punishment of me and I went to the place I go to when things get out of hand, the place where Mum and I are together, somewhere far away from him.

I never drew another picture after that day, I'd learnt my lesson. But what I was becoming had begun to bud, the soil of my mind a fertile place for darkness to germinate and take root.

I was slowly becoming the monster that Cat Box needed and it was finally calling me home.

WITH THE BOWSAW in hand and the satchel weighing heavy on my shoulder I shamble across the garden.

Henry my half-brother sat in the sand pit. He was a few years older than me, but he never acted like it. He's a bit simple you see, challenged some people say, a sixteen-year-old trapped in an eleven-year old's mind and outlook on life. Henry was born with his umbilical cord wrapped around his illegitimate neck from that harlot Sharron's womb.

Harlot. That's what mum called her when I heard them arguing one night, when Mum had finally found out about this whole other family he had, that was only days before she fled.

When I think about what I'm going to do to Henry I don't even feel bad about it because even God had tried to kill him once. Somehow, he'd survived that trauma and it was time for me to finish the job God had started so long ago.

He'd quickly become the apple of my father's eye, and I wanted to hurt my father in ways he'd never forget – and Henry was the way to his sealed-off heart. I'd mortally wound that bastard and not bat an eyelid whilst I did it.

Henry was the constant thorn in my side. He'd taken all of my father's love and I withered in their shade, neglected and left to fend for myself; a hanger on to a life my father longed to forget.

My father loved that blithering idiot of a child more than me. He'd spend hours playing with him and he'd never dream of marking Henry's flesh with his hands. Was it because he was simple and you simply don't beat the ill of mind? Was that why he took all his frustrations out on me, because I was better than that idiot child could ever hope to be? Was it because I was a child prodigy, gifted with words, numbers and art; whilst Henry couldn't even tie his own shoelaces? Or was it that he just loved his new life and his new family more than his old one, more than me?

Whatever the case I'd make him pay and the video would have what it craved.

A blood offering.
Someone you hate.

"Hey Henry, you wanna come with me to the woods?" I whisper to him.

"Is there bears in the woods?" He says, fear making his eyes large pools of brown.

"No bears, we don't have bears in England. So, you wanna come? I've got so many cool things to show you? Here you can even hold this if you like?" I held out the bowsaw, the rusted teeth glinting in the light, the patina on the blade already the colour of blood.

"Is it sharp?" Henry offered, his eyes big and wide.

"Yes, very sharp, I'll show you when we get into the woods if you like?"

"Oh, I'd like that Danny, I'd like that a lot. Can we cut stuff up with it?" Henry got up and stamped across the sandpit, treading on the castle he'd spent the morning making. He held out his hand, fingers opening and closing like a kid demanding cake.

"Here," I said, passing him the blade. "Now you just be careful with it ok, I don't want you cutting yourself."

"No. That would be bad, I promise I'll be good, I'll keep my beady eyes on it."

I relinquished my hold on the bowsaw and Henry held it aloft, his eyes staring at its hungry teeth, oblivious of the fact that those teeth would soon be chewing him up and spitting him out.

"Right, let's go." I said.

"Hang on Danny, shouldn't we tell Daddy where we're going?"

There was concern in his voice, but I was preoccupied with the bile rising in my throat at his use of the word *Daddy*. I begrudgingly swallow it back down because I know that soon it'll all be over.

A blood offering.
Someone you hate.

"No, we don't want to bother him, you know that he likes to sleep in on a Saturday... it'll be our little secret... yeah?" I drop the word secret into the conversations as I know it will play to his child-like mind, a secret is something children love, and between brothers it's something he'll want to cherish; to him it'll be an olive branch and he'll think we're bonding.

But we're never going to bond.

If anything, I'll be tearing us apart.

And nothing will be able to put us, or him, back together again.

"A secret? I like that, just between you and me? Thanks Danny, you're such a good big brother, I..." He ponders the words that are stuck in his mouth. I know what he wants to say, he was going to tell me that he loves me. I'm glad he doesn't, it would make what I'm about to do to him that much harder.

Henry casts a fleeting glance back at the house, still debating whether to go inside and tell Dad what we're doing. He's also still pondering whether to say *I love you.*

I breathe easier when I see him heft the bowsaw. He's staring at the teeth again, it's as if Cat Box is whispering to him through its jagged teeth.

For a brief moment I feel that he's succumbed to his childlike mind, and that he'll need permission from dad. I feel doubt reaching out to claim him, he's about to turn and head into the house, but turns back to me instead; a smile broadly puckering his chubby little face, the face only a mother – *a harlot mother* – could love.

"Okay Danny, let's go and cut some things up!"

We move towards the hole in the fence that backs onto the forest.

I lead my sacrifice to the waiting Cat Box as if he were Isaac and I

Abraham. A beautiful symmetry of biblical proportions is taking place before me, as he carries the tools for his own sacrifice. It's as if this day was written in the stars long ago.

I pause and let him go ahead. I follow him through the gap in the fence taking one final glance at our sleeping house to ensure no one sees us leave.

I come through the fence, take his warm hand in mine and we march on to his final judgement, but there'll be no ram to save Henry as there was for Isaac, because he's the spotless sacrifice for the slaughter and Cat Box will have what it craves most.

A blood offering.
Someone you hate.

"ARE WE THERE YET?" Henry's voice breaks the silence at our journey's end.

"Yep, we're here." I fan my arm over the pit of discarded rubbish.

"Doesn't look good. Doesn't look like you said it would."

Henry sits down on the edge of the crater, his feet dangling over the drop as he looks out across all the discarded filth. He places the bowsaw next to him, folds his arms across his chest and lets out a huff of disappointment.

I scan the debris, feel a longing I've not felt before.

There's a quickening of my pulse, the steady thumping of my heart, bloods deafening whoosh in my ears as my skin prickles with excitement at the darkest desires of Cat Box.

I jump down into the rubbish; the wasteland of forgotten things. A small landslide begins to tumble down into the crater's hungry maw, an appetizer before the main course arrives.

"Come on Henry, I've got something to show you, something really special."

"I don't want to. I want to go home, I want to see mummy and daddy…" the mention of his mummy makes me think of my own mother, out there somewhere, trying to survive, trying to live, free from the hands of my dad, but she'll never free from the clutches of Cat Box unless I do its bidding. Images assail my mind, the flickering visuals from the video of viscera and bone, and blood and rotting flesh. I see my mother's severed head screaming from within the box, the voiceover from the VHS screaming a bedlam in my head.

We'll kill everyone you love and have you watch.

I can't let Cat Box find her.

They'll make me watch her die.

I've already mourned her loss, I can't mourn her again, in the flesh.

I reach out and grip Henry's wrist, he tries to pull away but my hand is persistent, unmoving. When I glance down it looks like my father's hand. Henry's wrist a sapling in my grasp that I could snap at any moment, and I can't help but think I've turned into the cruel beast I've wanted to destroy for as long as I can remember. I will destroy him though, one aching cut at a time as I take all that he loves from this world and give it stinking piece by stinking piece to Cat Box.

Find the Cat Box, make the offering, leave the video, be transformed.

"Look, come on. There's something I really want to show you." I tug on his arm, pull him towards the lip of the crater, he wobbles on the precipice.

"You're hurting me." Henry tries to wriggle free.

"Don't you want to see the Cat Box?" I offer.

Henry's face transforms before my eyes, his awkward grimace gone, his chubby face suddenly angelic, hungry for what my words might mean.

"A cat?" He offers as I pull him into the crater with me. I steady him and dust down his trousers. I reach up and grab the bowsaw from the ground above.

"Well, it's a cat box, there might still be a cat around? Shall we go and see if we can find it?" I shoulder my satchel, hold the bowsaw out of his eye line, tug his hand as I stumble my way down the embankment.

Henry pauses, resists my tugging.

I turn, my hand clutches the bowsaw tightly. I feel my knuckles crack as I squeeze the metal handle, ready to strike if need be, it wouldn't be ideal but he can't get away; not when we're so close.

I face Henry, begin to imagine the unimaginable, imperceptibly I begin to raise the bowsaw, its teeth hungry to find his flesh, to taste the sweetest of offerings.

"What colour do you think it is?" He offers.

I want to say red, the pigment of your innards, but realise he's talking about the cat. I relax my hold on the saw, not now, not yet, but soon.

"I don't know, what colour do you think it should be?" I offer, pull on his hand, he begins to slowly walk down the incline with me, he's giving the question much thought.

"Could it be brown and white?"

"Yes, that sounds good, brown and white... let's go find him, shall we?" I turn and pull again, this time he follows my leading.

"Can we call it Nevaeh?"

"That's a strange name, why do you want to call it that?"

"It's Heaven spelt backwards." He offers simply as he overtakes me down the steep incline, running to the bottom.

It was as if he knew what awaited him at our journey's end.

AFTER AN HOUR of searching we found Cat Box.

It sat on top of the rusted washing machine exactly as it was in the video.

Cat Box was much larger than the grainy images made out.

Henry peered into the box, through the mesh of rusted metal and found it to be empty, but it wouldn't remain that way for long.

Only in fulfilling your calling and purpose can you shift the judgement from you.

Retrieving the VHS from my bag, I walk over to the sacrificial altar.

Place the tape on top.

It's time for someone else to discover its message.

I lift the bowsaw and use Henry's discarded shirt to wipe the blade clean.

I walk away to what awaits me in this new life and the beast that I've become.

I peer over my shoulder; Henry's brown dead eyes stare back from inside Cat Box.

It was a squeeze but I made him fit.

Find the Cat Box, make the offering, leave the video, be transformed.

THE YELLOW MAN AND HIS INSATIABLE HUNGER

There's nothing I hate more than visiting my Great Aunty Trudy's house.

Firstly, she's not even related to us. My parents had a hard time explaining to me when I was little where she came from or who she was related to, but that didn't stop them performing their civic duty of caring for the elderly.

That duty has now been bestowed upon me, because after my mother and father died last year in a car accident, Great Aunty Trudy became my burden.

She'd grown attached to our family like an invasive tumour. My husband stopped visiting her when she'd used an anti-semitic slur when referencing him in conversation. He was in the room at the time and lost his shit.

So, visiting and caring for her has fallen to me, and me alone. I couldn't just leave her, she had no one. She'd apologised about the slur, said the word was a term of endearment towards my husband, pleaded ignorance; but she'd never change her ways, just like all those indoctrinated old worlders who think they're allowed to say what they like because they've fought for our freedom or whatever.

We were stuck with her now, and were quite sure she'd drink our marrow dry if it ever came to it.

All we really knew about Great Aunty Trudy was she was of Roman Gypsy descent. That wasn't something she'd told us, it was something we'd picked up in conversations over the years. Little spilled secrets that tumbled from crinkled lips when her natural storyteller came out; usually when we were about to leave. Reading our tea leaves was another delaying tactic she'd employ which couldn't help but entertain.

But underneath it all, Trudy was a leach. She sucked on our time and finances like a newborn on a swollen teat. She was terribly lonely and she'd keep on reminding us of that fact; before, during and after each visit.

It got worse after her husband passed away. He had come back from the war (what was left of him), having lost a leg *over there* but a lot more than his leg got left behind in all honesty.

Great Aunty Trudy kept his prosthetic leg in the lounge, it must have been a strange way to keep him close, even after he'd died. It just never sat right with me as a child. The weekly visits I made with my mum all have the stain of that leg in the background. I can sometimes still see it, smell it, feel it; it was just always there like a bad tooth you couldn't help but tongue.

I'd never met my Great Uncle Reggie, he'd been dead for twenty years before I came along. Somehow, through that godawful contraption I felt that I knew the man. It would sit there at the end of the sofa, a wooden, leathery contraption, nothing like the prosthetics you see today. It was made at a time when you did your best with what you had. It seemed to encourage people to stare, to notice your missing appendage rather than trying to blend in. It was a horrific thing, with all its belts and buckles, it looked like something you'd find hanging from a wall in a sex club in Amsterdam.

It would just sit there on our visits, sometimes when my parents left the room I'd swear I could hear the joint creaking when I looked away from it. As if Reggie's ghost was straightening this phantom limb. Forever tethered to that final resting place. Who knows maybe he was? Maybe Trudy kept it close so she could converse with him on cold and lonely nights. Maybe she's trapped him there and that's why she never leaves this one room in her huge four-story house.

The leg was there today too.

I hated coming here as a child and I hate it even more as an adult, subjecting my own daughter to this torture. It seems like I'm repeating past mistakes, as if it's some sort of eternal damnation, a cycle that will persist until there's no one else for Trudy to feast on. It'll keep on going until she outlives us all, a never ending cycle of despair.

I lean forwards to check on my daughter. She's playing with her doll on the floor, too close to Reggie's leg for my liking. It hasn't come yet but I'm waiting for the day Trudy informs Jessica that it was once her husbands, a sly glint in her eye as she looks at where Reggie's head would be, as if he were sitting on the couch.

I turn back to Trudy, she's staring out the window. She does that more often now, no longer the cantankerous raconteur from my youth, just the shadow of a crazy old woman who's cheese has fallen well and truly off her cracker. She watches the world slip by her window like grains of sand from an hourglass and I wonder how may grains are left in the hourglass housed somewhere in that sunken chest of hers.

I glance down from the frail woman to the table in front of her. Three pound coins are in a line. They're for Jessica now, but they used to be for me when I was little. I'd get them as a reward for listening to Great Aunty Trudy when everyone else had left the room. The memories are not very clear, but I remember the sight of those coins used to fill me with an odd mix of dread, uncertainty and fiscal need.

Next to the coins are two chocolate bars, again for Jessica, but once they were for me. Not both of them, she was never that kind, I was only ever permitted to take one. I'd always have to choose, but the choice was always a dilemma and always a bloody disappointment, because whichever one I chose the chocolate would have turned to liquid; but a kid can hope right?

Like today, those chocolate bars would have been sitting in the sun all day, when I'd get out the front door my mother would make me throw it away. The thrill of it never faded, I'd always take one, hoping that one day I'd get to eat it. Jessica will also take one when our visit draws to a close, she always does; like mother like daughter. Our glovebox is full of those damn things.

But there's another item on that table which makes me heave when my eyes find it. It always does.

It's the plate. A bone china plate with pale, blue horses that canter its edge as if trying to flee. It sits on a stained knitted doily, the same one she's had since forever. It's full of little sandwiches, each one cut into a neat little triangle, but the same telltale signs are present now as they were then.

The edges of the bread have yellowed, curled away from the filling like skin from a necrotic wound. You could tell just by looking at them that they'd been sitting in the sun for hours. It's the filling that makes me gag as it weeps from the bread like pus; warm and putrified. If it ever mistakingly reached your lips you'd feel the heat radiating off it like an infection.

I'd been offered one when I was a child, after my mother had left the room. I didn't know any better and I ate it without a second thought. I remember to this day the bone-dry bread, rough against my lips and the warm fish paste oozing out, coating my mouth with its muck. That's why I've warned Jessica about it. Told her under no circumstances if I were to leave the room, was she *ever* to eat one of those weaponised, breaded-missiles of salmonella.

I glance at the clock, soon it'll be time to leave, and I hope Trudy doesn't try to delay us this time. I stand, dust down my trousers and move towards her table; she turns, sees me motion to Jessica that we're leaving and suddenly her brittle voice breaks the silence.

"Oh, are you leaving so soon?"

"We've been here most of the afternoon Trudy, I'll need to get

Jessica home, get some dinner down her neck and then ready for bed."

"I've food right here," Trudy leans forwards, her skeletal arms reach for the plate from Hell.

"Won't you stay a little longer? She can eat one of these and that's half the battle won."

I nudge the plate away and I feel my stomach churn with my close proximity to the poisonous sandwiches.

"No, honestly Trudy, I'll need to get back, Derek hasn't seen her today and he'll want to get some cuddles in before bedtime."

"Oh. If you must then. This place just doesn't seem full anymore."

"Full?"

"You know, of life."

"Oh."

"She's so much like me you know?" Trudy nods to Jessica, who's inched closer to the ghost who sits in the corner, where at any moment I expect Reggie's leg to kick out because she's gotten too close.

"How so?" I humour her.

"Well, she's got my hair hasn't she."

It was true, I'd not noticed it before, tight black locks framed Jessica's pale face.

"She does, doesn't she."

"And she's got my nose too, there's no denying it."

As she says the words, Trudy reaches up and strokes the hooked beak hanging from her face. Trudy must know we're not related; that there's no chance of Jessica sharing any genetics with her, but I just nod slowly at the coincidence.

I reach out and grab her cold cup of tea.

"A refill for the road?"

Trudy licks her puckered lips, struggling with her words. She's forgotten to put her teeth in again.

"That would be lovely, thank you darling. It's not at all true what they say about you."

I don't dare ask who or what, for I know this will only delay our departure; so instead I take the cup and head to the kitchen. As I turn to leave, I hear her voice again, this time with more vigour than before, as if she's grown excited.

"Jessi?" She says. The sound of her voice, coupled with the fact she called Jessica by that pet-name grates the last of my resolve. I glance at Jessica who peers up at me briefly, catching the stern look and slight head shake, and I know from her subtle reaction that she understands not to eat the sandwiches. Trudy will try and make her; she always does at this point, but Jessica will say no, and make her excuses as discussed.

"Come to your Great, Great Aunty Trudy, I've got a surprise for you."

I decide to leave Jessica with Trudy; she'll be okay. What's the worst that could happen? I made it out alive. Jessica will be fine.

I step into the kitchen, boil the kettle and return moments later. As I walk in I catch the tail end of a conversation.

"So you'll say hello if you see them?"

I place the cup down and hear Jessica's reply.

"Mummy says I can't talk to strangers."

"Oh that's good," Trudy continues. "And rightly so, but these aren't strangers, they're Great, Great Aunty Trudy's friends."

I ignore the conversation, place my arm on Jessica's shoulder and begin to manoeuvre her toward the door.

"Well if they're your friends then I guess that's okay." Jessica replies sweetly. I note the pound coins are gone; I'm not even going to ask about the strangers. Maybe I'll ask Jessica in the car, or she'll ask me. I lean forward, and give Trudy a kiss on her wrinkled forehead. It's cold and I half expect my lips to freeze to her head like two pink petals.

"Same time next week Trudy?"

She turns and stares out the window.

"It's so lonely here, can't you stay a little longer? They're all leaving me, all the time."

I grab my bag, I've no time for these mind games.

"Next week it is. Come on Jessica."

Jessica picks up her doll and Reggie's leg twitches involuntary and tumbles to the floor. Jessica picks it up, stares at it before placing it back down in the indentation on the sofa. I had been about to scream when Reggie's leg sprung to life but I realised quickly that Jessica's doll's hair had somehow gotten caught in one of its many buckles.

"Jessi," says Trudy.

I half expect Trudy to regale Jessica about the leg, but as she turns we both see that she's pointing to the chocolate bars on the table.

"You didn't pick one."

I turn to Jessica and nod towards the table. She scampers over and observes the two chocolate bars intently, The excitement on her face grows as she picks up the purple wrapper and it wilts like a dead flower. I watch her face, crestfallen, as she realises it'll end up in the glovebox with the others when we get outside. Jessica kisses Trudy on her wet and toothless mouth, which makes me shudder. I hold out my hand and Jessica skips over to me. She's safely back within my motherly embrace where nothing bad can ever happen.

"See you next week Trudy." I offer in a sing song voice, but all I get is a grumble as she reclines in her seat and peers out the window, preparing to watch us drive away.

WE'RE NOT EVEN twenty yards down the road before Jessica starts talking.

"Mummy?"

"Yes darling?"

"You know that really old game you and Daddy talked about, Pac-Man?"

"Yes, the one with the yellow head that eats everything?"

"Yes, that's the one. Great, Great Aunty Trudy says that Pac-Man comes to visit her."

"Great Great Aunty Trudy said that?" I wish we could cut the *'greats'* but Jessica will insist so I play along.

"Well no."

"I don't think she's even heard of Pac-Man has she?" I offer.

"No. She hasn't. I asked her but she said she'd not heard of him, but it's what I thought of."

"And why were you thinking of Pac-Man?"

"Well when you were out of the room, she asked me if I'd ever seen him?"

"Who?"

"Pac-Man."

"But you just said she didn't know who Pac-Man was, so what did she actually say?"

"The yellow man."

"*The yellow man?*" I reply quizzically.

"She said that he comes to visit her, more fre...re..quently now that the ghost have all left."

"Ghosts?" I say, as I almost swerve into oncoming traffic. I can't believe what she's filled my daughter's head with. I turn right into our road, already knowing that tonight will be sleepless.

"Yeah. Ghosts. But she said there aren't anymore left so he's been biting her."

"Biting?"

"What does feasting mean Mummy?"

"Feasting? Well it means eating... why?"

"Great, Great Aunty Trudy says that it's been feasting on her head, on her thoughts and..."

"That's enough, Jessica!" I peer into the rearview and Jessica's face is shocked. I rarely raise my voice to her, she's a good child, the best.

"Sorry Jessica, I... I just don't think we should be talking about these things so close to bedtime. We'll talk about them tomorrow if you still want to, but not now okay?"

"Okay Mummy." Jessica utters as she turns to look out of the window. I turn the ignition off and she doesn't move, I glance up and catch her profile, she looks so much like Trudy it makes me shudder.

"Was that what you were talking about when she said saying hello to her friends?"

"Yes." She offers quickly.

"Right."

"But you said I can't talk to strangers."

"That's right." I say before I open the door and step out.

"So, I can't talk to them? Even if they're Great, Great Aunty Trudy's friends?" Jessica says before I close the door, she doesn't hear my words as I make my way around the car.

"Especially then!" I say softly before opening her door and escorting her from the car. Tonight, I know will be a sleepless, hellish night.

JESSICA'S DOOR opens and I'm suddenly awake. It's dark and so I check the clock; 1:32am. Suddenly my door swings open. Jessica's feet pad softly to my side of the bed; she's learnt to come to me as her father would sleep through the apocalypse.

I feel her hand on the covers, and notice her wet eyes, she doesn't know I'm watching her.

"Mummy?" She whispers slowly, drawing out that one word so much it lasts five seconds.

"Jessica, what are you doing out of bed?"

"I can't sleep."

"The more you walk around the more awake you'll get."

"But Mummy..."

"Jessica!" I raise my voice to a harsh whisper, "Go to your room."

"Can't I stay here with you and Daddy?

"No. We've spoken about this, just go back to your bedroom and you'll fall asleep soon."

"But it's too loud."

"Don't be so silly. What's too loud?"

"It is, it is, it is!" Jessica's voice skips like a lyric on scratched vinyl.

"Jessica! I've had enough, I knew that bloody... that Great, Great Aunty Trudy would have spooked you with all her nonsense. Go back to bed, close your eyes, and fall asleep!"

"But there's too many people in there."

I feel my chest tighten as I bolt out of bed. Pushing Jessica aside I stomp to her room. Half-way there wishing I had brought Derek's bat. I hit the light switch, and no one's there. Just a room full of cuddly toys and clothes strewn across the floor. I turn to Jessica at the door.

"Oh," Jessica says after examining each of the corners. "They must have all gone."

"Who?"

"Great, Great Aunty Trudy's friends."

"The ghosts?"

"Yes. The ones she said would come and say hello. They wouldn't talk to me; they looked really cold, all blue and shivering and their breath, it was like little, white clouds tumbling from their mouths."

I put my arm around her and usher her back to bed. She jumps in and I tuck the cover around her tightly. It's cold in her room. I glance at the window, it's closed and so I turn back to Jessica.

"What did they want? Great, Great Aunty Trudy's friends?"

"They didn't say, they said they had to go; that the yellow man would come looking for them. They said he would know what Great, Great Aunty Trudy told me, that he would find them if they stayed too long and they didn't want to get me in trouble. They said he was a bad man."

"Pac-Man?"

"Yes. They said he would be angry that I brought them home with us."

"You brought them home?"

"Some. They were in the car with us and the others followed us all the way home. Didn't you know Mummy? Did I do something wrong?" Her lip quivers.

"No. No, of course not darling, I'm sorry for shouting at you, I didn't know, I wouldn't have made you come back to bed if I'd known, but you say they're gone?"

Jessica checks the room again.

"Yes. They're all gone."

"Okay sweetheart, now they're all gone, why don't you go to sleep. Mummy's going to be just down the corridor like before. If they come back you make sure you come and get me right away and I'll tell them to stop waking you up!"

"Okay Mummy. Night night!"

I stand, lean down and kiss her on the head, notice that her crinkled brow has smoothed out, the tears gone. She yawns as I make my way to the door. I turn, smile and turn off the light. The unicorn nightlight becomes the only source of light in the room. As I pull the door closed Jessica speaks again.

"What if Pac-Man comes Mummy?"

"Then you come and get me right away and I'll give that mean old Pac-Man a thing of my mind, and if he's not careful we'll set Daddy on him." Jessica laughs, "Sweet dreams, darling!"

"Night Mummy, I love you!"

"Love you too sweetheart."

I pull the door shut and walk back to my room, knowing that she'll wake me again, she always does when she has bad dreams.

"Hey... hey... wake up sleepy head!"

Derek's voice pulls me from my slumber. The curtains are open and the early morning sunshine streams into the house like a home invader, unwelcome and uninvited. I peer up through slits of eyes and he's got a cup of coffee for me. I shimmy onto my elbows and lean against the headboard.

"You've been sleeping like the dead."

"What is it?" I know him so well, somethings not right.

"Well I just got off the phone with the hospital."

"Hospital? Is..."

"Jessica's fine, she's still asleep. You must have been awake a bit in the night judging by that luggage you're hauling around under your eyes."

"Yeah, she was up pretty early, but I got her back to bed, who was on the phone?"

"Sorry... it was the hospital, Trudy died last night."

"Trudy? Our Trudy?"

"Yeah, they said she must have fallen over, hit her head on something hard, probably that bloody sandwich table. They said her skull was fractured; she had a bleed on the brain. She didn't suffer. They'd said she was probably dead when she hit the floor."

"Dead?"

Derek places a comforting hand on my leg. He thrusts the coffee in his other hand towards me, this time I take it.

"I'm sorry darling. I know you didn't really get on with her but she was family?"

"She wasn't family Derek and you know that!"

"Well, yeah but..."

"Did the hospital say anything else?"

"No. Just a freak accident. She was so frail a stiff breeze would have knocked her over. Nothing anyone could have done."

"Did they say what time?"

"I think they said it was about 2am, why?"

"Nothing it's just…" My mind wanders *2am was a little after the ghosts left Jessica's room.*

"Where's Jessica?"

"She's in her room, I let her sleep in."

I place the coffee on the bedside table, my thoughts racing like wild horses. Derek stands back, lets me pass. With each lumbering step I take towards Jessica's room the temperature drops; my skin breaks out in gooseflesh. I don't know what to expect.

I extend my shaking hand and push the door open. It's dark, her curtains are still drawn and it takes me a moment to make out the haphazard shape under the covers.

I scream.

I scream until I can't breathe.

Derek runs to my side, I pull away from him and fall to my knees, staring at what remains in the darkness of her room.

All that's left are bits and pieces of Jessica the Yellow Man couldn't stomach.

EVEN DEATH CAN'T SEPARATE US

Belinda's been sick for a while.

Her warm, shallow breath carries more than just her sickness, it carries the unmistakable stench of death.

I stroke her pallid clammy face and my fingers find their way to her head, her hair between my fingers is brittle like steel wool and wet from the fever she's been running.

Belinda hadn't told me she was ill; she'd kept it a secret, but she can't hide anything from me for long, because I know her intimately. On this occasion she decided to keep quiet, because if they found out we'd have been kicked off the caravan. There was no space afforded for sickness to spread. She'd never allow us to be thrown off, because after thirty-seven years we'd finally found a place to belong, together.

A strange little family to call our own, they'd accepted us warts and all.

Although Belinda was ill, she'd been able to work through it and although the others hadn't noticed, I had. It wasn't something visible, onlookers would never have noticed. It was something that I felt deep within me, an unease that made my flesh crawl, as if it threatened me somehow.

I've always known when Belinda hasn't been feeling well, we're connected in ways others aren't; a closeness nothing can replicate. Belinda's pain somehow becomes my pain, her fears become my fears and her anxieties become my anxieties. We've shared everything, even a man, once.

We share a special bond, a deep-rooted connection that comes from being twins, inseparable in many ways since birth, a tethering formed within the darkness of a cramped womb that will never be broken.

We've watched each other grow, seen each other date, laugh, cry, grieve; even get married (Belinda not me), and as crazy as it sounds I'd even watched her consummate her marriage from beneath the sheet I was hiding under. As I've said, we're closer than most sisters could ever hope to be.

When that marriage failed due to my constant presence, I was there to help Belinda pick up the pieces; holding her hand and soothing her after the miscarriage that soon followed. Even then it appeared there wasn't enough space for another life to grow between us.

But the caravan keeps rolling as it always does. We've another town to visit, the next one being Juniper. We've townsfolk to entertain and a small fortune to be made. Juniper we've heard is a shit hole; apparently we'll fit right in.

I touch Belinda's hand, it's cold and clammy. I whisper to her in the dark.

"Belinda, it's me, are you okay?"

She returns my question with a string of weak grunts. She's in pain, I can feel it deep within my tissue. I stroke her face again, she's so cold now; the fever long since vanquished but the rankness of her breath persists. It's soon diffused by the breeze and replaced with the stench of the caravan we call home; the sour odours of the lost souls that surround us, a thick and suffocating miasma that settles like a dirty blanket on our skin.

We hit a bump and the caravan tips before correcting itself violently. Belinda begins to slip from our bunk, and I try to hold on, to pull her back, but soon I'm tumbling too, her dead weight pulling me with her. We land hard in a haphazard stack of limbs. In the dark I wonder which bits are mine and which are hers. If only she'd speak or move I'd be able to distinguish which bits belong to her within the irregular shadows.

She feels numb, our connection no longer a living thing, an arm gone to sleep, a heavy weight hanging dead by my side.

It's as if the fall has severed our lifelong bond.

Grunts of disproval ring out, shortly replaced by shifting bodies on threadbare mattresses and squeaking bunks. Our companions try to get back to the sleep they were so rudely forced from and as they fall silent; I'm aware of the low din that underscores our journey, the wheels of the caravan that never cease in their eternal quest for money.

Something's wrong.

There's an ache within my core, a pain that has coiled itself around my organs like a python, constricting me from within. People say twins are telepathic, that if one hurts, the other can feel their pain; and maybe that's true.

Was the pain that woke me Belinda's?

What isn't she telling me?

How bad is the sickness that festers within her veins?

The initial pain I'd felt radiated through me as if I'd been branded; a hot poker plunged deep into my innards where it seared and sizzled.

I realise now that it wasn't the rankness of Belinda's breath that woke me, it was the pain deep inside that made me cry out, an agony that tore me unforgivingly from my peaceful slumber.

I look up from our position on the floor. Moonlight from the barred window sheds some light and I can make out the crude dimensions of her head. I scoop the curtain of hair from her face, and suddenly wish I could put it back.

I scream until there's no more air.

Belinda's dead.

My head swims and I sense a poisoning within my tissue. Her dead blood swims through my veins now, polluting and destroying the stricken vessel I've become. A body that clings to life but is so close to death I can taste its bitter tang on my tongue.

There's a thumping sound; a broken heart attempting to pump blood to extremities no longer accepting it. Each beat in my chest trying to revive pieces of me that have so suddenly ground to a halt.

But the banging is not my heart, it's the frantic thumping of our concerned traveling companions on the caravan wall, loud petitions as they scream for the caravan to halt.

The horses neigh as the driver pulls back on the reigns. I feel the juddering of the wooden wheels skidding on gravel as he brings the caravan to a full stop. Nothing stops the caravan, but as far as I'm aware no one has ever died in here before. As I stare down at Belinda I hear the grunt of disproval from Harold as he jumps down and swiftly makes his way to the back, his feet crunching angrily in the gravel.

He's mad, but I don't fear him now, I fear nothing, because I've lost everything. The latch on the door lifts with a rusted whine before it slams back down on the wooden doors that pen us in.

Harold pulls the doors open.

"Someone better be dead or dying in there..." He starts with his usual bravado before the rest of his words stick in his throat like swallowed glass as he takes in the scene before him. Moonlight floods our rank dwelling and reveals Belinda, my beloved sister; stricken on the dusty floor, dead.

Harold nudges her with the toe of his boot and I want to scream, but I choke the words down, for it would end in a beating, one I'm not sure I'd survive. He pulls a rag from his pocket and places it over his nose as he crouches down, hovering over us.

"Get them out!" He shouts, muffled by the handkerchief.

My heart dropped in that moment and I began to sob, knowing what's to come.

"Did I stutter?" Harold stands, his shadow looming over us. "Get them out, one's no use without the other. Who's going to pay to see that."

I reach out, attempting to protect her in death in the ways I was unable to do in life. She doesn't deserve this treatment, neither of us do.

"Now!" Harold snaps, "We've got a schedule to keep!"

Slowly from the shadows come the freaks, the people we've grown to call family.

Their hands descend on Belinda and begin to raise her off the floor.

Marissa's sorrow-filled voice comes softly to my ear, the mother we never had. Her wispy beard makes her an oddity but her unconditional love erases it from where I'm looking.

"Can you stand Mary? We can carry Belinda, but you'll need to walk." Her arms reach under mine which are holding tight to Belinda's body. The rest of the tribe lift and carry her sagging form from the caravan, while my body follows as it always does. I stay close, because I have to, but I feel weak. I stagger and Marissa rushes to assist.

As I feel the cold night air on my skin the sensation sends chills deep into my marrow. I glance at the feet ahead of me, scurrying us into the night. I'd look up but the weight of Belinda's dead body holds my head down.

"Over there!" Harold croons from somewhere behind the conclave. In the moonlight I can make out yellowed grass under our feet and a bit of a decline. I slip but Marissa keeps me upright. We descend further until we're in what appears to be a ditch.

"That's far enough." Harold says from on high, directing his minions below. "We need to be in Juniper by sun-up. Leave them!"

"But –" Marissa utters, turning to confront Harold; but she's cut off before she can plead our case.

"Don't you go getting ideas, Marissa or you'll be joining them. It's the same for all of you if you get sick or die on the road. There's a reason it's called a *freak's burial*. Now drop them and get back in, or you'll walk the rest of the way!"

I hear Harold move away, his grunts of disproval resonating in the still, humid air. Marissa leans in, whispering so no one else will hear.

"I'm so sorry Mary, but we have to go, with any luck it'll pass quickly, I pray it does, for the both of you."

Suddenly I'm pulled to the ground by my dead sister, our heads forever fused together. I hear the feet of our family walking away accompanied by the muted sound of whispered prayers. I think I hear Marissa sobbing, but then it's gone consumed by the dead of night. The doors to the caravan creak open before slamming shut. The chains jangle against the wood before Harold thrashes the reigns, the crack they make is quickly followed by the clip clop of hooves.

When the night falls truly silent, I speak.

"It's okay Belinda. You and me, together until the end, just how we always imagined it."

I pull her cold hand closer, rub it gently with my thumb to wipe away the tears I've spilled on her skin. I kiss her hand and feel her death coursing through me. It won't be long until she pulls me with her, forever leading the way, but for now, I wait.

A smile breaks across my face as I realise that we're alone but together.

And not even death can separate us.

THE GREAT WITHERING

The boy was flung into the restroom wearing nothing but a dirty loincloth. He tripped due to his uncoordinated, tired legs, landing awkwardly on the ground. The tanned skin of his back crisscrossed with reddish welts, wounds which were healing in aggravated pink scar tissue.

He remained on the floor, breathing heavily, his back expanding and contracting, his ribs showed with each laboured breath, he was seriously malnourished. The scarred skin of his back rippled like a fish's scales in the harsh, clinical lighting of the bathroom. He scanned his surroundings quickly, looking for some place to hide, his eyes huge with fear, they were desperately trying to locate a place he'd be safe and hidden.

The door to the restroom flung open again and the boy turned his head; his long, brown and matted hair hung over his face like a dirty veil. His bright, green eyes peered through the follicle curtain and alighted on the figure skulking towards him, a tormentor with vengeful determination in their stride. The young boy braced himself for what was to come – he gritted his teeth and prepared for the stinging taste of the ASP on his skin.

The hulking figure stood before him, his shadow loomed over like a tower. In a well-practiced routine he flicked his wrist and the telescopic baton appeared from thin air, as if he were a magician and this act of torture his sadistic sleight of hand. The sound of the baton forming made the boy flinch before it had even touched his skin, but touch his skin it would, there were guarantees in life; birth, death were two of them and the third was the sharp sting of the ASP. The man raised the baton and brought it down with a whip across the boy's already scarred back. The force of the blow drove all the air from his lungs, he collapsed onto the cold tiles with a guttural moan. The floor, snow cold against his skin, and the frigidness of it made him feel alive, albeit for a second, but he hugged the tiles because he needed to feel something, anything to remind him that he *was* still alive, that they hadn't killed him – yet.

The boy placed his slender hands on the floor and began to lift his skeletal frame from his prone position; he knew from experience that if he'd stayed down, if he gave up, it would only earn him more lashes with the baton. And so with trembling weak arms and a few ragged breaths he began to rise. He breathed through the burning pain that shot across his back, he'd been burnt by them during their experiments so he knew the feeling intimately, but he'd also suffered much worse at their hands. There was always a chance the situation could spiral out of control and match those torturous beatings if he remained apathetic to his plight, and so he continued to rise from his grounded position.

A boot soon connected with his stomach which lifted the boy from the ground. He was momentarily weightless before he fell back down to the cold tiles. From this new position he reached out his arms, gripped the water pipes from the hand basin and pulled his way under the porcelain shield of the sink, narrowly missing another attempted swipe from the ASP. Once under cover, he pulled his legs up to his chest, going foetal in an effort to protect the soft and delicate parts of his body from the beating that was to come.

"You dirty piece of shit!" the man spat as he charged toward the boy. He swiped the baton down again and again, the sound the ASP made as it cut through the air was a sharp whistle, each swipe ended in sickening, dull thumps as it connected with the boys arms, legs, side and back. The man was furious in his desire to destroy the boy; the keychain at his hip jangled a merry tune throughout. The blows rained down until the man grew breathless and red-faced, his uniform now marked by dark rings of damp under the arms and his shirt had become untucked around his rotund gut. He stowed the baton on his belt next to his gun and keys. He tucked himself in and straightened his uniform before he stared down at the wounded boy on the ground, raised welts and thin cuts decorated the boy's already puckered back in a latticework of torment. The man stared at the fresh carnage he'd caused, a mirthless grin peeled across his blotchy and sweat-riddled face before he raised a hand to his mouth and wiped the creamy spittle that had formed in the corner with the back of his hand. He hawked a chunk of phlegm from his throat, and spat it at the child before him, the marble of green and yellow catarrh landed on the boy's back with a splat before it began its slow descent, trickling over raised cuts and welts.

"That'll teach you for pissing in your pen, you disgusting little pig. We should have left you in that shit-shack of a village to starve like the rest of mankind. You got ten minutes - piss, shit, tidy yourself up and then I'm taking you to dispatch – it's almost time for transport!"

The guard checked himself in the mirror and ran a hand through his thinning hair. After he ensured his comb-over covered his bald patch, the hulking man turned away from the bloodied and broken boy at his feet. His rubber-soled shoes squeaked on the floor as he turned and departed, not before he shot one final glance over his shoulder at the specimen that quivered on the floor, he was making sure he'd not killed the pathetic child, *Riddick* and *the project* would not be pleased if he had. The boy squirmed and with a sigh of relief the guard shook his head at the thing before him and left, leaving the boy to lick his wounds. The door closed and trapped the boy within a new prison.

The child took a moment. A long pause to ensure the man wouldn't return and beat him down again, which was often the case. When he was sure the guard wasn't coming back, he rolled over and got onto his knees. With shaking, skeletal arms he reached out and clutched the edge of the basin. Pain coursed through his body, he winced as the cuts on his back opened wide with the sudden movement. He pulled himself up, placed both hands on the rim of the sink and paused. He lifted his gaze; his green eyes peered through his sweat dampened fringe at his reflection in the mirror. He turned away from the mirror to observe the deep cut on his upper arm.

The child watched intently as tiny fissures, green and vine-like in texture wriggled free from within the bloody laceration. Vines climbed out of the gore like weeds desperately struggling towards the sun. His eyes darted to the wall, when he noticed the shadow that was cast by his body. Tendrils danced in the shadow, and he realised that his back was alive with the roving fronds that twirled out of his sliced dermis like naked branches in a winter sky. He shuddered as they moved independently around his body, as they tickled his flesh with their fussing.

His eyes returned to the deep gash on his shoulder. Green shoots reached across the wound and embedded themselves into the healthy untainted tissue, before they burrowed into his flesh like a needle and thread. He looked on fascinated, as his skin was pulled closed from within, as it knitted back together; all that remained was the pink scar of fresh growth. A clear secretion oozed from the wound on closure. He reached his hand up and dipped his fingers in the substance. It was tacky, honey-like as he rubbed his coated fingers together. He lifted it to his nose, sniffed, it smelt sweet. He poked the tip of his tongue out and lapped at the resin, he needed to be sure that it was the same as last time. His face screwed up with the flavour in his mouth, there was no denying that it was sap. It tasted of honeysuckle. The boy peered into the mirror before he turned, desperate to see his back, although he knew what he'd discover but he had to be sure, after contorting his body he saw the fresh wounds across his back had been sealed, the skin also coated in the same syrupy secretion. *What have they turned me into?* he thought, as he peered at his haunted face in the mirror again and wished he was back home in his village, back before the bad men came to take him away and experiment on him.

Back to when he was a boy – before they made him a bomb.

The boy could smell a strong odour of mould. It filled the room with a thick choking miasma. He tore his gaze away from the mirror and padded around the room in search of the stench. The fragrance was cloying, as if unseen hands were intent on pulling him towards its source. He tasted the earthy mushroom notes in his mouth. He staggered towards one of the closed toilet cubicles. He pushed it open and the stench smacked him in the face as he wheeled back as if struck. He ventured forwards, glanced inside the toilet bowl, nothing. He scanned the floor, again nothing. His eyes slowly rose to a tiny window near the ceiling, where he noticed the moon. *How long has it been since I've seen the moon?* the boy wondered, as he edged further into the cubicle.

The smell was thick, his mouth watered. He felt something ripple under his skin, as if the vines that had crept out were maggots that burrowed beneath his dermis, where they feasted and festered in darkness and blood. He glanced down as the sensation pulsed through his arms and noticed the veins on his forearms had grown engorged; the vines or was it sap pulsated towards his hands in rippling waves. His hand raised all of its own volition, his fingers splayed as if he were trying to stop something charging towards him. His fingers tingled as his hand trembled in the air, pressure building in every digit.

He soon noticed the mould. Dark splotches had accumulated in the corner of the rotting wood of the window frame. It was the source of the stench. With his hand outstretched, directed at the mould he watched as the small cluster of fungus began to spread like ink on blotting paper. It feasted on the wood in moments, the timber splintered and ruptured in the frame. Fungus bloomed, and then withered, as if a whole season had happened in the blinking of an eye. Fresh growth again blossomed from the mulch left behind. Plant growth soon manifested from the loam, small shoots appeared first then they quickly morphed into thick, thorny vines which pressed and scratched against the glass. Suddenly there was a crack; the pane of glass shattered but each jagged piece was caught by the green hands of flora that appeared.

The boy felt the cold night air for the first time in years, as it settled on his skin, he felt both lost and found, and with a sinking feeling in his stomach he also felt terribly alone.

This was the moment he'd been dreaming of, the chance to escape the *bad men* and their experiments, he could be free at last – but what was left of the world he'd been torn from all those years ago? What was left of his village in India? He'd heard the other children that came after him talk about the fall of the world; the riots, the pollution, rising tides, and global warming. But what pained him most was the talk of mass deforestation to ensure the cities didn't fall. But the cities did fall, but not to lack of fossil fuels (although they were now in short demand), they'd become the birthplace of pestilence and the epicentres around the world for the *Great Withering* as the guards often referred to it. The boy wondered if his village would still be standing or if it had gone the way of the *Great Withering* too; the hope that filled his heart wounded him gravely and tears fell from his eyes, carving clean tracks through the grime on his face.

He tore himself away from reverie as he noticed that the vines had formed a hedge ladder from the window to the ground, steps that he could ascend and escape. He peered once over his shoulder at the door, half expecting his tormentor to rip him from this sweetest of moments and return him back to the labs and the tyrannical and vicious perversions of Riddick, the *very* bad man. But no one came.

He turned back to the cubicle, and stared up at freedom in the shape of a broken window. He could fit through that gap now; the vines had removed some of the bricks and the hole now tailor-made for him, and him alone. The boy stepped tentatively forwards. He climbed the ladder quickly, and then jumped down from the hole in the wall, finally he was outside. He choked as he breathed the outside air, it tasted foul, it was thick with smoke and choking fumes. He peered up and in the distance he noticed fires raged in what he imagined were once cities and towns and woodland.

He pulled himself up and lent against the brick wall. He leaned into the shadow as searchlights roved the concrete wasteland he now found himself in. Sheltered in the dark, away from the cruel eyes of the guards in their kill towers, the tendrils appeared again. This time they emerged from his mouth and nose, his teeth shifted in their moorings, his nose tickled and he thought he would sneeze as vines crept up and out of his nasal cavity. The green barbs pierced through his gums, anchored themselves to his lips and nose, where they formed a latticework of foliage. It soon began to restrict his breathing. The boy panicked, his hands gripped at his throat and then his mouth, as he attempted to tear the fibrous growths away. He feared choking and suffocation, but he feared most making it this far only to fall by his own enhanced mutation. But as he struggled with the vines he soon realised he could breathe, that the mesh over his mouth wasn't choking him but filtering the smog-filled air he breathed. Taking a deep breath of clean air he closed his eyes and imagined he was far away from here, back in his village, back with his family.

He was torn from his thoughts by the sound that emanated from the bathroom window; he craned his neck and lifted his ear to the broken window above. He could hear the slow, squeaking footsteps of his tormentor. The guard was back in the room stalking his prey. '*Your prey's long gone*' the boy thought with a smirk, before the deep baritone voice from his nightmares ripped any joy from the moment, and the boy soon realised that getting out of that room was only the start of his escape.

"Come out, come out wherever you are?"

There was a bang as the cubicle door was kicked open and clattered against the wall, the sound echoed into the night like a gunshot. The boy stood still, his naked back pressed up against the brick wall.

"What the actual fuck." The guard's voice rang out into the night.

The boy didn't move. From his position he scanned the concrete jungle that had replaced the actual jungle he was used to, a chain-linked fence about three hundred meters circled the camp. The ground between the fence and his position was lit up every few moments by searchlights; the boy didn't have time to study their pattern, to find a way through the puzzle of beams. It suddenly dawned on him that although he was outside, he was a long way from free.

He flinched as the booming voice hit him again, his panicked eyes returned to the window, but he knew the guard would never be able to fit through that hole, and when he'd climbed down the ropes of vegetation had crumbled to dust once he'd made his exit. But he still needed to stay out of sight in case the guard peered out.

"Riddick, come in Riddick," followed by a hiss from the guard's radio, "We've a situation with London, come in Riddick."

London? The boy thought. Memories of the pens invaded his mind; he could see the other children in their glass boxes, their scared faces stared back at him. Each pen had a name above it; Rome, Helsinki, New York, Istanbul. They were some of the places that had succumbed to the Great Withering, there were more, and the boy knew this. He'd heard hushed conversations, seen diagrams and maps in the laboratory too, each showing a city that needed to be *re-pollinated* with life - *I must be London?* The boy mused.

"This is Riddick, what is the situation with London?"

"He's escaped, sir."

"Escaped? How the hell did he manage that?"

"There's a hole in the lavatory window, sir, seems the boy climbed out, there's.... there's signs that his mutation is active, sir."

"Of course it's active, he's due to be detonated – need I remind you that our investors are expecting delivery of London today?"

"Sir... no, sir. I'll find him. He couldn't have gotten far."

"Good, because if you don't find him... well let's just say the joint council won't be happy, the investors will be baying for blood, they'll make an example of you, do you understand?"

"I understand, sir. I'll trigger the alarm."

"The fuck you will, soldier. I don't think you understand, we've got the eyes of the world on us right now and I don't want to raise a panic on the eve of our maiden voyage. The walls are now closed around London. The chosen are in place, *everyone* in the London Ark has paid a great deal to be there for the first re-pollination. And you, losing London on the eve of that great spectacle, when the world is watching and praying for an end to the Withering... shit. The investors will not be happy GODDAMNIT! Find London and whatever you do don't raise the alarm, we want to project the sense of calm here, do you understand?!"

"Yes sir. Sorry, sir."

"I haven't got time for apologies, just action, now find him, or it's all our heads on the block."

London heard the guard grunt in anger then a fist slammed into the cubicle door. London flinched again, imagined that hand finding his flesh as it had so often. He listened intently and heard the man's feet squeak away from the window. London glanced around the camp, he was still pressed up against the wall in the shadows; he'd observed the area ahead before making his escape, as he pondered which route he'd take, London heard the radio cackle to life again.

"The pens? Are the pens secured?" It was Riddick again, his voice tinged with worry.

"Yes, sir. I believe they are?"

"Make sure London doesn't get to the pens soldier, he may try to free the others. We, and when I say we, I mean you, soldier, need to ensure that we secure the other assets. If London escapes and you better pray that he doesn't, we don't want him leading those vessels away with him and detonating all over the wastelands; it'll make a mockery of the programme, this programme is for chosen, it's not for those that live on the fringes of society in those withered shit-stinking places, do I make myself clear?"

"Crystal, sir."

"But if he does escape, we'll need to spin it as an exercise gone wrong. But if he should become nullified in his escape, we'll just supplement him with another; we can't keep the chosen waiting. The other children might not be ripe yet, but their extinction event should bloom new life nevertheless, just on a less grander scale. So make sure you lock down the assets first, before you fuck anything else up."

"Roger. I'll check the pens and ensure the resources are locked down."

"Don't fail me, soldier."

London listened intently to the silence that followed. He could hear the soldier's harried breathing which was replaced with a cry of rage as he slammed the door to the restroom and left. London knew that now was the time for action. He steadied himself against the rough brick and breathed through his mask of moss, the filtered air became somewhat of a tonic to his addled mind, thoughts tumbled like a rockslide; he could run, should he run and get as far away from this place as possible, would he make it, how far would he get before a searchlight found him and a bullet tore him down. It was the pens that kept him rooted to the spot; the children, most of them younger than him, and their eyes, haunted orbs that pleaded for help. Their innocent faces pained him gravely. He needed to do something to make this right, and in a moment of clarity he realised he needed to fight.

London's arm prickled as he surrendered himself to rescuing the children in the pens; he glanced down and discovered his forearm was crowned in purple thorns that ran along its edge, each barb emerged from his dermis through a slit of flesh that glistened with the sap that coursed through his blood. The thorns hardened in place, each one thirsty for the taste of revenge. He noticed that his fist had changed colour, it was now purple and white, his knuckles bloomed into a gristly club, but organic in nature, prickly barbs appeared and he realised it wasn't a club but the head of a mighty thistle. Armed with the weapons that nature provided London strode in the direction of the pens, he had no option other than to fight. Someone had to free the children from the experiments and the evil intentions of man and money.

Nature was fighting back and London would be its willing soldier.

THE FIRST GUARD was dispatched with ease. Blood dribbled down London's arm; each thorny barb coated in ichor and flayed skin which had peeled away from the guard's throat in stringy ropes like pulled pork. London hadn't wanted to resort to violence, but something deep within propelled him to take a life, as if the Earth's vengeance needed fulfilling and he was the vessel chosen to release its wrath upon those that wanted to harness its ways for the few.

With the guard's key card in hand, London let himself into the pens. An eerie quiet met him as he made his way through vacant tunnels and experimentation rooms. News of his escape yet to have been passed down the line, but they'd be aware soon enough; and so he quickened his pace. He peered over his shoulder as he approached the bulkhead door leading to the pens; He paused, peering into the darkness. When nothing appeared, he swiped the card. The panel on the wall turned from red to green, the doors hissed open. London half expected to find soldiers on the other side, guns and batons raised ready for attack, but there was nobody there, only glass pods and the haunted faces of children that had been subjected to the unthinkable and the unimaginable.

London stood before the child whose destination, and new name he assumed, was Helsinki. She sat at the back of her cell, cloaked in darkness, her pale arms wrapped tightly around her legs; she rocked, lost in her own torment. He tapped on the glass. Helsinki raised her head, the fear in her eyes soon dissipated to what he assumed was hope as she crawled from the darkness on hands and knees, towards the glass that separated them. London placed his hand flat against the pane, Helsinki reciprocated and there was a connection, not with their hands, but in their plight as they studied each other. She smiled at him. They were one and the same and their mutations made them brothers and sisters in a new age. London watched on as Helsinki's smile stretched further and further, her mouth splitting and peeling back at the corners, her skin fraying like a torn plastic bag as the top of her head fell backwards. Glistening white shards sprouted from her bottom jaw and as her head flipped back, more of the barbs sprouted from the other half of her mouth. As the two halves of her head yawned open they swayed like two large petals; the gore it revealed glistened wetly and invitingly – it was horrifically beautiful and London couldn't look away. Her head had become a humanoid Venus Flytrap. Her head quickly snapped back, the shards of tusks slipped back into their moorings and London watched as tendrils of green began the work of affixing her mouth back in place. He smiled, gesticulated that he would be back. Helsinki pleaded for him to stay but he needed to check on the other children before it was too late.

Rome stood before London, his mutation was visible unlike Helsinki's and his own, they could hide their gift but the sight of the boy pained London greatly as he knew there was nowhere in the world Rome could hide without the corporation finding him again. Rome's eyes were deeply set in a dark pillow of flesh, masked in soft fuzz. London watched as the boy shook his head vigorously; the fine fuzz drifted away from his face and floated around the cell. Rome's naked head was a blackened bulb; two white orbs stared out from a slab of darkened skin. London watched as new seeds sprouted from his skin. Within moments the boy's head was covered again in dandelion seeds. London knew the seed pods that drifted in this boy's cell showed the exact reason the corporation had him captive and were prepping him for detonation, each seed a kernel of hope and the promise of regeneration, or as Riddick had delicately put it, re-pollination.

London checked the other cells; there were seven children. Eight cities including him had been highlighted as the first to receive re-pollination, but he knew it would never end there, especially when the world witnessed London's detonation and re-pollination in action, they'd clamour to be next. He knew they'd hunt down more special children, they'd subject them to tests and torture, tearing them away from all they'd ever known for the ongoing quest of money and the survival of the rich and those deemed worthy. The poor weren't allowed to thrive, they'd been left to fend for themselves in the hinterlands after the Great Withering – the only purpose they served was a neck for the chosen to rest their aching feet.

London reached for the key card and brought it up to the terminal. He flinched as something stung his neck. Suddenly his moss mask started to deteriorate; it turned to dust and crumbled away to the ground. He lifted his hand to his neck, his fingers feeling for the source of the pain. He pulled the object he'd discovered from his neck and held it between his fingers. His vision grew cloudy, he shook his head to clear the befuddlement, when it swam back into focus he realised he held a dart. Glancing up he noticed a wall of human shapes in the distance, one stepped forward and even though his vision was impaired he knew it was him, his tormentor, back to inflict one last atrocity.

London prepared himself to fight, but soon staggered on legs that didn't feel quite his own. He placed a hand out to the cell next to him, steadied himself before he succumbed to the tranquiliser and collapsed to his knees. The figure loomed over London as it often did before it crouched down and pressed the tip of his ASP to London's already aching chest, he pinned London to the floor and ended his feeble struggles. London knew it was over.

"Riddick. Come in, Riddick."

135

"Yes. Do you have an update on London?"

"The payload has been secured and nullified. He is ready for transportation."

"Get him in a pod and start the preparations, we've a timeline to keep and we're already behind thanks to your stupidity. Don't fail me again."

"Affirmative, sir."

London was lifted from the floor by two guards. His head lolled back and through the haze of his failing vision he noticed the children of Mother Nature screaming from their cells, each of their mutations bloomed and reset as they mourned the fall of their would-be saviour. Unceremoniously the guards dropped London into a waiting pod, as he fell into the cushioned interior he couldn't help but think it was his coffin. The soldiers closed the transportation pod, as London stared out of the glass. As they sealed him inside, they also sealed his fate, and with an aching feeling of dread he knew that there would be no coming back from this.

London was in a new prison, scared for what was to pass as they took him for transportation and later detonation. Deep within his core London felt oddly at peace, although he was scared he knew that nature would find a way to survive, it always had. The children and London were a testament to that. As the freezing fog filled his chamber for transportation, and just before he gave into the drug-induced sleep, he closed his eyes and prayed he'd live long enough to find out if that old adage was true. If nature would indeed find a way.

A DISTANT SILENCE

I've grown to live with it, the bewailing.

The constant bedlam that contaminates every waking moment. My brain slowly becoming spoiled soup within my skull.

Some say they can see the future, figuratively speaking of course. Or you've the bastard charlatans who *pretend* to see it, making money off the backs of the easily persuaded and weak-minded.

My affliction's a curse, a constant white noise.

A pandemonium of fighting, screaming and incessant pleading.

Unlike the others, I can't see the future, I *hear* it.

But today the voices fell silent.

A year from now, there will be nothing.

TWO BEASTS, ONE MASTER

Everyone has two warring beasts within them, and one always wins out.

They're part of us, coiled around our cells, embedded deeply in our genetic makeup. These beasts are so ingrained you can't just cut them out; it's what makes you, you, and what makes me, me. It's our free will that decides which one we serve, which one we allow to breathe, and in the end which one gets to see the light of day.

Whether it's the addictive and vindictive beast or the loving and compassionate one; there's only room for one to rule.

The beast doesn't stand on ceremony to be welcomed, it's already here, waiting, lying dormant – ready to emerge. Some people say it's nature vs nurture, but they'd be wrong. It's Darwinism; survival of the fittest, the strong will overcome, whilst the weak will be consumed.

The first time my beast emerged was when my son threw his food on the floor.

138

MATTHEW SAT in his high chair, stuffing steamed broccoli and mushed-up fish into his chubby little mouth. I was cleaning the dishes and my wife was taking a much needed nap. Matthew had been running us both ragged of late, but I could escape for the day with my work, but Jennifer was here all the time, we'd decided it best she hit the sack and I'd feed the boy.

I heard the plastic plate hit the floor and when I turned Matthew was smiling at me. I peered down and noticed the fish and broccoli strewn across the living room rug.

I lost it.

I flipped out.

I pulled my hands from the soapy water, and marched toward him, his smile lost instantly, withdrawn by his chubby face as the hulking beast approached. I picked the plate up silently, all the while glaring at him. He knew something was wrong, but had no idea what I was about to do.

"You ungrateful little sod. Don't you know there are people in this world that don't get to eat?"

The words coming from my mouth sounded familiar, as if I'd heard them before. I picked the broccoli from the floor, scooped up the fish and mashed it all back onto the plate, noting the many pieces of carpet lint and crumbs giving his fish some added seasoning.

I don't blame him for what he did next, but the little swine tried to knock it off the table again. I'd not have eaten it either, but that was beside the point. The beast forced me into action, it needed to show its dominance. *It* was in control of my actions now.

"Eat it."

Matthew shook his head, kicked his legs and threw his head back in frustration.

"Eat it," the beast repeated.

Matthew's chubby hand grabbed a piece of broccoli, raised it to his mouth and then threw it across the room. He laughed, he thought it was funny, but it was anything but to the beast.

"EAT YOUR DAMNED FOOD!"

I screamed into his frightened little face. I heard Jennifer stirring, then our bedroom door opening, quickly followed by her frantic padding toward the living room. I leaned forward shooting Matthew a look that could curdle milk. These were the precious moments before I'd be emasculated and so the little sod needed to *know* who was boss.

"Fine, you don't want it then you don't eat it... you'll go hungry, you little drama queen!"

Jennifer entered the room and looked at me like I was a stranger trying to steal her child. I shook my head as she ran to comfort our son. I stomped over to the bin, stamped on the peddle and the lid slammed against the wall.

'Mummies boy," I said under my breath as I scrapped the remains of his food.

Suddenly a searing pain lit my wrist on fire. I peered down at my hand and watched the skin begin to bubble and wither; it split, and reddish-pink fluid spilled from the torn flesh as the skin peeled away from the joint. It crinkled like crepe paper, unfurling over my hand to reveal a rougher dermis beneath, a different shade from my own, liver spotted and with grey hairs instead of black.

The skin hung on by the tips of a few fingers, reminiscent of a dying leaf clinging to a branch in winter. I shook my hand and the offending skin floated down and landed on the rubbish within. Slamming the bin closed I stood still and inspected my new, old hand.

"What on earth are you doing?"

Jennifer was staring at me, and I held my hand up; but her face registered zero surprise.

"What?" Jennifer said.

"Don't you see it?"

"See what?"

"My hand?"

"Darren, don't be an idiot, you can't hide what you've done by feigning injury. Own it, you were wrong. I'm so ashamed of you right now; don't think I didn't hear you calling our son a Mummies boy. You sounded just like your father!"

I stood aghast. She'd wounded me with her words, she knew it was a low blow.

I let my arm drop, she'd tried to reach out and hold my hand, to bridge the chasm she desperately wished she hadn't opened.

But she couldn't close the gap or hold my hand, I wouldn't let her. The words had lodged themselves in me like arrows, and it would take time to get over them, it always did.

I wanted to scream that I was nothing like him, that I'd never be like him, but I couldn't find the strength. The truth of the matter was, I couldn't deny it. It was like *he* was speaking through me, using my tongue to form those cutting words. *His words.*

I didn't speak; although there was much I wanted to say. If I did I knew that my words would split her open like a cat o' nine tales, so I let it slide. Instead, I skulked around and retired to the bedroom to lick my wounds. She left me to it, as she'd done so many times before.

THE SECOND TIME the beast emerged was a year later.

I'd gotten home to find Jennifer waiting at the door, a bag slung over her shoulder. She couldn't wait to get out the house.

"I'm meeting your sister at the shops; she needs a bit of retail therapy and well so do I. You'll be alright with him won't you?""

Jennifer leaned in to kiss me on cheek. I could tell she still didn't trust me around our son, and it smarted like a wound doused in vinegar. I glanced down at my hand, the old skin still present, the hand that wasn't mine but the beast's. Jennifer glanced down too, but as I'd come to learn, she couldn't see it. It was my cross to bear, my wound to carry; a reminder of the toxicity within.

"It's fine, where is he?"

"He's playing in his room, been in there for a while now, he's content so just let him play. I've made him dinner, it's on the side."

Jennifer grabbed her keys and walked out as I stood in the doorway and watched her leave. I could hear Matthew talking gibberish down the hall and things were good, but I could tell she was nervous about leaving. I waved and she struggled to smile, it was more of a grimace I observed as she disappeared from view.

Grabbing a beer I made my way to Matthew's room. I could hear him muttering nonsensically to himself, having the time of his life, and I felt today was going to be a good day.

Pausing outside his room I lifted the beer and noticed the tainted flesh of my hand gripping the bottle. I took a swig and then lowered it, moving the bottle to my other hand so I wouldn't be reminded of *that* day with each sip.

I opened the door to discover Matthew twirling around in the middle of his room without a care in the world, and wearing a princess dress. He stopped dead in his tracks as my bottle hit the floor, the beer glugging out and disappearing into the carpet. I couldn't hide my discomfort; the hand was burning again. Suddenly Matthew's eyes began filling with tears, his bottom lip quivering as he witnessed the disappointment on my face.

"Take it off!"

He stood there shaking, I stepped into the room.

"Now! Do you think I'm joking with you?"

"But Daddy, I like it."

I reached forward, my beast hand was burning as I grabbed hold of the dress, the feel of sequins and silk beneath my fingers sickened me. Matthew went to step away but I held tight. As he struggled the dress ripped down the middle.

"Daddy you've ripped it."

As I took hold of his snivelling, little face the beast rose within me, and before I could choke the words down they were out.

"Are you a sissy?"

He didn't move. Didn't say anything. Just stood there mute. I hated it when he did that.

"No son of mine is going to wear a fucking dress. Take it off. Boy's don't wear dresses!"

"No. I want Mummy!"

"I said take it off, SISSY!"

I reached forward to rip the garment in two when my flesh all but caught on fire; a burning sensation radiated within my chest, stealing my breath in an instant. I fell to the floor, and began writhing in agony, a snake trying to slip its skin. Matthew hurdled my prone body. I tried to grab his foot, drag him down, but I missed. He ran screaming from the room and hid somewhere in the house. He'd left me and I don't blame him; at least he was safe, for now. Twisting in pain I rolled over onto my back, tore my shirt open, the buttons flying in all directions.

I looked down. My skin was constricting, my ribs protruding, the ache in my chest almost certainly a heart attack. Inexplicably I could smell sulphur and singed hair. My hands pawed at my tender flesh, and small tears began to appear, minute stress fractures in the dermis. The skin browned at the edges before it began to shed, crackling, turning to dust and ash as it crumbled away on my frantic, panting breaths.

Blood and pulsating muscle were underneath, bulging veins crisscrossed my torso and yellow ligaments showed between my bone-white ribs. I writhed as my flesh cooled, realising it was slowly turning the colour of my hand; the new skin aged and discoloured, my bare chest was covered in tufts of grey hair. Moles I never had before had appeared, and there was a scar from someone else's appendectomy which graced my stomach.

That night I slept on the sofa. I tried to tell Jennifer what happened but Matthew interrupted before I had a chance to explain. He'd told her all about me calling him a 'SISSY' and nothing I said mattered after that. It was pointless; she was right and I was wrong, so why argue?

143

THE FULL METAMORPHOSIS happened a year later. The beast that I'd been housing and was destined to become finally emerged.

Jennifer asked if I'd be okay to look after Matthew, a funeral wasn't any place to be taking a child. I said I'd be fine, and we both believed it. It'd been a long while since my last outburst and I was feeling better, lighter. I felt as if I had it under control; the skin didn't haunt me anymore, and besides no one else could see it anyway.

I awoke to the sound of Matthew's door opening. Silently I rolled over and watched my door. Matthew's indecisive feet were padding around outside, I could tell he was scared of waking me. The door swung open, and the bed dipped as my son climbed in. He crawled over the duvet, assumed I was still asleep. I reached out and turned on the lamp. The room burst with light and we both squinted until our eyes adjusted.

Matthew sniffed, his eyes red. He'd been crying, and just sat there amongst the covers, eyes down, fearful, hands in his lap fussing with a stuffed bunny. I reached out and placed my hand on his leg, not the beast hand, the other.

"What's wrong sport? Did you have a bad dream?"

He shook his head and cuddled his bunny tighter before lifting his gaze, eyes brimming with tears. He nodded, and looked down again, averting his eyes. He'd been doing this for weeks now, waking us up with nightmares, crying, ensuring we all lost a good night's sleep.

"What was it this time? A monster under your bed?"

He shook his head.

"In the cupboard?"

He shook his head again.

"Behind the curtain?"

Again the same.

"Well come on what was it?"

He peered up at me, timid and afraid. I saw his lip quiver and watched as he worked out what he wanted to say.

"It's Mummy."

"What about Mummy?"

"I dreamt... I dreamt..."

He was visibly shaken, but I had no time for pandering.

"What? You dreamt of what?"

"That... that she... died."

As the words left his lips, the tears started to fall.

"Stop it. Stop crying. Mummy isn't dead... it was just a bad dream."

I shook his leg and tapped it in a *there there* motion. Still the tears fell.

"Stop it. Matthew, stop it!"

"I... I... can't!"

His body was wracked with sobbing, his breathing short and sharp, his nose running a slug trail to his lip.

"You can and you will!"

It was then I felt the beast rising and I couldn't do anything to stop it.

"What have I told you about crying?"

I sat bolt upright and the beast's hand reached out and began shaking Matthew's shoulder. He was but a ragdoll in my grasp and he squirmed to get away but the hand wouldn't let him. It had a mind of its own. I leaned in, my face inches from his.

"Only girls cry Matthew. Are you a girl?"

He shook his head.

"You sicken me,"

He whimpered, and I raged.

"WHEN WILL YOU GET IT INTO YOUR THICK HEAD THAT MEN DON'T CRY!"

As the spittle flew from my mouth I felt a sudden and searing pain tear through my face, as if branded by an iron. I screamed like a wounded animal.

I lifted my hands, pawed and patted at my face as if trying to put out a fire that wasn't there, yet somehow my face was raw and blistered. When I pulled my hands away they were covered in dribbling flesh, strings of gory skin – like melted cheese – connected my hands to my face. I peered out through the webbing of flesh and fingers and saw Matthew sitting stock-still on the bed, his snivelling had subsided, he was watching me suffer.

"Daddy, are you okay?"

I rolled from the bed, my hands holding my face together so it wouldn't slip off. I pressed and moulded the remains of my face to where it had sluiced before staggering half-blind into the bathroom. I removed a hand to open the door and watched as pieces of my face dribbled through my fingers and spattered against the tiled floor.

"Daddy?"

I slammed the door behind me, turned the lock and sealed myself within. Lurching towards the sink and the mirror above it, I was suddenly fearful of seeing what I'd become.

My face oozed in gelatinous ropes into the sink. I placed my hands on the edge of the basin, blood dribbled from my fingers, snaking its way to the plughole.

"DADDY!"

Matthew was banging at the door, his voice a mixture of concern and fright.

I could smell burning flesh, a foul, cloying stench. Tendrils of smoke began to obscure my vision as if it were desperately trying to hide my new face from me as it appeared through the haze. My forehead suddenly pulled tight and I felt my cheeks hardening, my lips didn't feel like my own.

"I'm sorry Daddy!" Matthew shouted from the other side of the door and my heart ached for him.

I reached with the beast hand and turned on the tap; the water washing my shedded dermis down the drain.

I stood in front of the mirror a new creation and as the smoke cleared I realised I'd become what I'd always feared I would, but was powerless to stop.

A smirk spread itself across the new landscape of my face; the beast was pleased at last.

"I won't cry again daddy. Only girls cry!"

His voice sounded different.

It sounded like me when I was his age.

My father's face stared back at me and winked, a cruel sneer puckering his ugly mouth, which was now my mouth and my ugliness.

"Hello son, did you miss me? I always told you the apple doesn't fall far from the tree... right, let's have some fun!"

BEAUTIFUL ATROCITIES

"Don't ever leave me Tyler."
"I wouldn't."
"I mean it. Don't even think about it."
"What's gotten into you lately?"

"Nothing, just know that if you ever did, if you ever left me, I'd find you and I'd fucking kill you!"

And so, I stayed. Although everything within me told me to run; to get as far away from her as possible. I stayed because I loved her, but mainly due to the fact that she *would* find me, and when she did she *would* kill me.

I watch her from a distance.

It's best to keep her that way. Distant. Keeping her like this ensures that she can't sneak up on me and I'm also far enough away that I can flee at a moments notice.

I've learnt my lesson over time, paid for it with a broken wrist and four cracked ribs; stared back at myself in the mirror more times

148

than I can remember with her deposits of hate adorning my skin. Black eyes, split lips and finger-shaped bruises around my wrists and neck.

Her anger is her gift to me, whereas my gift to her is my art.

Every time I draw her it leads to the same outcome. A belittlement followed by a beating.

What tortured people we artists make.

Over time she's become infuriated by my art. I should really liken it to a curse as nothing good ever comes from it.

It might actually be a personal affliction. A suffering I crave without ever knowing why, but whatever *it* is, I'm drawn to it again and again like a dog to its vomit.

It's become clear over our time together that she doesn't ever want to see what I see – how I see *her*.

I think it's because in all my depictions of her she can't help *but* see the darkness staring back at her from the page or canvass I've daubed her image on. She only ever sees the broken person she hides so well. She'll never fully understands my art, or the beauty I conjure from her being; the strong, loving, vulnerable and deeply troubled woman I've grown to love with abandon.

It's true what they say, beauty is in the eye of the beholder, and if she can't understand her beauty, how am I to show her it exists.

She carries many demons, some of them in the physical scars that decorate her body; the delicate crosshatchings of self-harm and the ruddy slashes of a knife that glorify her supple arms and stomach. Her skin is embroidered with pain and suffering which shimmers like fine jewels. But there are other scars too, ones that don't shine so brightly, the ones she's scared I'll discover. Deep-rooted wounds stored in the grey tissue of her mind, abysmal lacerations that never heal but gape wider with each passing day and troublesome voice in her head.

I think she hates me because in my art I put her vulnerability on show for the world to see. She's reminded me many times with the cruel works of her hands, that the one thing she is not is vulnerable.

She's powerful and vicious. But she's also my wife. My darling Christina. And I love her deeply.

THE FIRST TIME Christina saw one of my paintings of her she'd beat me so badly I couldn't leave the house for a week. She'd severely broken my nose to the extent that I looked like a pugilist who always finished in second place. The black eyes that bloomed were the colour of a Francis Bacon painting at first; purple and even deeper, darker blues. After a few weeks the bruises shifted into a more Van Gogh palette and I was able to leave the house without drawing too much attention to myself.

She'd been furious the first time I showed her who she truly was and I should have learnt my lesson. Christina had taken the painting and punched a ruddy great hole through the canvas. I imagined she was picturing my face on that canvas instead of hers.

"It's disgusting!" Christina had spat as her hand burst through the canvas before she flung it to the ground. I'd peered up from the painting at her feet and stared dumbfounded at her anger at my love of her. Saliva hung in translucent ropes from her chin, reminiscent of a rabid dog waiting to bite.

"But I did it for you, to show you how beautiful..." I'd managed to get those few words out before she turned on me, wide eyed and insatiable; eventually pummelling me seven shades of Bacon, and smearing my nose across my face like a piece of wet clay.

The first time's the one you remember most.

The first times a charm they say.

THERE WERE other works of art that followed but all went the way of the first.

After the initial beatings I'd sworn that however bad it got, however much she'd beat me, she'd not ruin my love for her; or destroy my other love, my art.

How foolish I was.

The beatings quickly grew in their intensity. Christina took great delight in crushing my mind, body and spirit. She'd wreck me before sticking me back together with declarations of regret for her actions and promises of getting help and getting better.

But she'd do it again and again, she couldn't help herself. It was an addiction, one that had no cure unless she was willing to face the demons that ravaged her soul and showed up in the images I drew of her.

My love for Christina eventually waned over a long period of time. I resigned myself to the fact that I couldn't help her, couldn't reach her. She was adrift in her own sea of despair and pain. The only thing keeping her afloat in those choppy waters was her dark desire to destroy me and subsequently the beauty I created.

I'd cower regularly in her ominous and overbearing shadow. I was a houseplant, neglected and left in the dark to succumb to its circumstance. I'd become limp and pathetic, a version of myself I despised. I longingly craved any ray of hope that might reach me in my personal darkness; some fleeting hope that she might have changed because I was desperate to drink again from the fountain of the love we once shared. But our love was gone and would never return, and so over time, I slowly gave up the fight to free her from herself however much it pained me to do so; instead I focused on my own survival.

She'd stripped me of everything I knew to be true and just. She'd beaten me, emasculated and humiliated me, but there was one thing she could never take nor break and that was my art. If I'm honest with myself if there's one thing in this world I couldn't live without – it wasn't Christina, although I feel great shame in saying that. My art was freeing and I longed to be free.

I needed to be free.

So I sit here whilst she sleeps and I draw.

I know she'll hate it because it shows her as vulnerable and weak and she's never such things as I've already mentioned. But I desperately want to capture this moment, showcase her for the thing that she is when she's not awake, when she's not my tormenter. I know if she were to wake and find me sketching she'll ask to see it, demand to see it; I'd be forced to submit myself to her tyrannical rule or run the risk of the pain that quickly follows a rebuttal.

If I'm being honest with myself I actually want this piece of art to wound her. Savage her in ways I could never do myself, and so I'll hide behind my art, let it speak of my frustrations to the beast that prowls this house. I'll let the pencil mar her in ways I could never dream of.

The pen is mightier than the sword people say, but the pencil cuts cleaner than any scalpel. The pencil always gets to the heart of the matter, it doesn't merely scratch the surface, it cuts clean and deep; opening up the things unseen.

As I finish the sketch I hear her treacherous voice leak into my head like a deadly dose of radiation, polluting and spoiling my resolve.

"You've got no talent!"

I place the pencil down.

"Why do you bother?"

I unclip the paper from the board.

"You're just wasting your time."

I hold the sketch out in front of me, it quivers in my shaking hand. How I tremble at her rebuttals.

"I've seen children's finger paintings that are better than that!"

I grab the paper between both hands and crush it into a ball. She's won again without even speaking a word, because her torment of me is a song on repeat in my mind.

I hold the ball of paper crushed within my fist.

Christina screams.

I turn and notice that her body is now a hideous ball of entwined flesh. Christina's limbs are wrapped around her as if she's become a human straitjacket. Her legs are pulled up into her chest, all twisted and broken. I can't make out the rest of her appendages as they're mangled and tightly coiled around her body like a scarf made of meat, nothing of her is where it should be.

I take in the repugnant vision before me and stifle a gag. Her bones protrude from her body in all the wrong places. Her limbs are bent where joints shouldn't allow such movements. Her head is sunken and now resides further down in her chest cavity, where ivory horns jut out from her chest; surrounding her face like a crown and it takes me a moment to realise the white barbs are her ribs.

Her hate-filled eyes glare out from within the mangled pretzel of her body, her stretched skin a crude tarp that barely contains her protruding and shattered bones which threaten to break free from their coverings.

What have I done?

I hear her muted groans from within the contorted ball of flesh. I take the paper and slowly flatten it out on my leg. Her body flips and twists and unravels before my eyes. Sickening wet pops sound in the room as her bones find their way back into the sockets they were rent from moments earlier.

She's returning to her old self, but not quite. The pieces don't fit back together as they once did. When I tear my gaze away from the thing that used to be Christina I notice that the creases on the paper align perfectly with the broken woman who lays before me.

Each crease of the paper mutilates her flesh with broken bones and puckered flesh. She tries to speak but the lungs that lay in her chest are now redundant, two punctured beach balls that will never inflate; her ribs having torn them asunder on their way through and out of her chest. A hideous wheeze grows louder within the cramped confines of the lounge and the sound is maddening.

Her eyes find mine and hate burns brightly within them. She

doesn't speak, can't speak. She's unable to suck in the air needed to formulate and utter words, but her gaze tells me everything I ever need to know.

"I'll find you and I'll fucking kill you!"

Picking up my pencil I return it to the drawing. Christina watches on, her eyes growing wide as the pencil hovers above the paper. She's wondering what I'm about to do to her. I carefully ponder my next stroke and wonder how it'll lead to her eventual demise. I don't even know where to start with the broken thing before me. I twirl the pencil around in my fingers whilst I weigh up my options.

Should I strike her a mortal wound, puncture the paper with the pencil where her heart or brain would be, put her out of her misery once and for all. Or should I enjoy my torture of her, the way she enjoys her torture of me. I pause before pressing the rubber on the end of the pencil to her foot on the page. I'm curious to see what happens. I begin to rub the marks away and as I do, I glance up to witness the work of my hands playing out on her appendage and I smile.

Christina's toes crumble into the soft arch of her foot. The slab of meat which remains recedes further as I rub, it's as if her calf is swallowing her appendage. There's no blood, just a faint dust that falls to the floor as her foot crumples away to nothing and I let the rubber enjoy its meal.

I glance back to the page and move the rubber to the other foot, I peer up at her. She shakes her head as best she can, is she telling me to stop? Or is her body succumbing gradually to the shock that ravages her. I smile back. A pitying smirk that's full of malice and pent up aggression before I slowly began to erase her other limb; taking with it her means of travel, her way of finding me when all this is over. I let the eraser feast with abandon, I watch on as her leg withers to nothing but a stub that matches the other ruined leg; both ending mid-way down the thigh, crude amputations at the very best.

A groan of disproval emanates from her lopsided mouth which is now a cavern of teeth; broken and twisted and red because a crease lays across that gaping hole on the page.

I stare at her godawful mouth and remember how many hate filled words have tumbled from that stinking orifice. Words that burned and blistered, cutting remarks that maimed and held me a prisoner. I can't stand her nonsensical babbling any longer and so I move the pencil to her mouth. Christina's eyes bore holes in me as I flatten out the paper and manoeuvre the rubber near the pencil outline of her mouth. She shakes her head furiously at me.

If her back wasn't broken with the ruddy crease that carves the paper across its middle I'm sure she would rush over on her stumps and pummel me afresh. Her murmuring reaches me one last time but with one quick stroke of the rubber, I remove her voice instantly. Her lips smudge across the page and with another swipe they're gone entirely.

I lift my gaze and bask upon the smoothness of her actual face. The skin over her mouth is one solid piece of flesh, but as she screams the skin pulls taut, her cries of anguish remain trapped within. The nubs of her teeth appear under the puckered skin as if she's attempting to bite through her own gag of flesh. At least for now I've silenced her. Her belittling words forever trapped in a prison of skin and bone. She can feast on her own words of destruction and poison, she can damned well choke on them for all I care.

I settle into the chair and peruse the paper in my lap before my eyes dart to Christina, deliberating where I should continue my torture of her. Although she's silent I notice the utter contempt and hatred she has for me; anger still brews for me in her eyes like a storm trapped within a bottle. I can feel the condescension she has for me from across the room; she despises everything about me, but most of all, she despises my art, which it turns out this time, will have the final say.

I spin the pencil around in my hand, a well-practiced routine when making my art. Slowly I bring the nib to the page. Christina jerks around uselessly in her prone position, her stumps of legs kick about like a petulant child. She's desperate to flee the beautiful atrocities I'm inflicting on her body. I press the nib on the paper and she mumbles in pain behind her fleshy gag.

I begin to draw.

I glance from the page to her face as I go, I don't want to miss a single moment of her annihilation.

I sketch a rose growing out of her eye. Peering up I witness the thorny stalks bursting from the succulent bed of her pupil. Sharp thorns feasting and ravaging her orbital meat as they emerge from her eye in shredding, green tendrils. A cruel, grey, gruel trickles wetly from the flower bed of her eye socket; slicking her face in grey water as if it were a canvas being primed. The rose begins to bloom as I sketch the petals on the page, unfurling from thin air. Pleased with my work I start on the next eye, extinguishing her sight with the beauty created by my own hands.

She lays there sightless and voiceless, my tormentor finally laid low.

I take my pencil and place it to my lips. I peer over at her as my mind races away with all the possibilities that remain.

"You'll never lay another finger on me again," I shout.

I remove the pencil and using the rubber I slash it across her arm. Her actual hand tumbles to the floor. I slash at her other arm and another thud rings out. I glance down and both of her hands are on the carpet, opening and closing like giant, dying spiders. Turning my attention back to Christina I notice her arms flailing around, both ending at the wrists. She was a useless thing now and I smiled at taking her hands. I see her filthy appendages fidgeting on the floor, as if they're still hungry to find me, ravenous with the intent to enact one last atrocity on my flesh before they're gone. I won't let them, I can't. I grab the rubber and remove them from the page. With her weapons of torture finally gone I feel a great unburdening prickling its way up my neck as my head fills with hope. I'm almost free.

With the realisation that she can't hurt me with her words, hands or feet; I smile.

"But what to do with the pieces of her that remain?" I question myself as I take in her pathetic form.

She no longer has eyes to scold me with, no mouth to spit her spiteful rhetoric, no hands to harm me and no legs to chase me.

I'm finally free of her, but why do I not feel sated.

I glance at the wreckage of her and I feel sorry for her in a way. To leave her like this would be an abomination, and deep down I love her too much to leave her like this, to have devastate her so completely.

She doesn't deserve this fate but then again neither did I.

I'll show her mercy where she showed me none. I'll show her love in her final moments where all she ever gave me was her utter contempt. I'll provide her with a way out of this nightmare even though she doesn't deserve it, and I'll do it because it's the right thing to do. I'm not a bad man, I'm just a desperate person trying to survive the monster that he loves.

I'll put her out of her misery and hopefully in doing so I'll be spared any more of my own.

I scrunch up the paper, watching what's left of Christina's body fold in on itself. She's much smaller now and the remoulding of her body happens almost instantaneously. The roses now twist in and out of the fleshy folds of skin-coloured soil they bloomed from. Green thorny vines snake around her broken and twisted limbs like Japanese knotweed, choking what little of her life remains.

I lift the ball of paper to my mouth because it's the only option I can think of at such short notice. She'll always be a part of me whether I'd like to admit it or not, so I might as well keep her with me, for all time and on my terms. I bite a chunk out of the paper and begin to ingest my beautiful atrocity. Piecemeal by stinking piecemeal.

I stare at Christina as a chunk of what used to be her vanishes in a fine sprinkling of dust. Bite marks appear in the conjoined mounds of flesh on the sofa. I chew the paper and feel it turn to a paste, when she's tenderised enough I swallow her down. The lump of congealed paper that used to be her slides its way down my oesophagus and tumbles into the darkest parts of me.

I take another bite and then another.

I feast on the beast until she's nothing but a sliver of paper held between my thumb and finger.

I peer over to where the last pieces of Christina reside. All that's left is an ear, part of her nose and a sprouting of hair; all attached to an indistinguishable chunk of flesh.

I wrap the final pieces of her into a small ball and finish my meal.

Reclining in my chair I rub my hand over my bloated stomach.

For the first time in years I finally relax, savouring the sweet taste of freedom on my tongue.

STORY NOTES

S tory notes I feel are important as a reader but also as a writer, they help to detail the creative process; and by reading them we find out where the stories we've just devoured originated from and how they may have developed or been refined over time. I feel they give the reader a glimpse behind the curtain and for a moment they can step into the mind that spawned the nightmares they've just consumed.

I also feel there is something deeply honest and open about detailing a stories inception to its final resting place, because some of these stories have travelled the various paths of submissions calls but never made the cut. But that's okay (honestly it is) someones slush pile is another persons gold. If you believe in that story, that's all that truly matters at the end of the day. Keep creating art people, keep writing for you, that's all we can do.

You can make beauty from the ashes of rejection, trust me, I know.

This outlook I have over rejections has not always been the case. There was a time early in my writing career that when I received a rejection I'd take it personally. It would play on me for days (possibly even months); feelings of inadequacy would flood in and it would be followed by a loud voice that screamed "You're not good enough!!!"

But now, after many rejections over many years I've grown to not be derailed or offended by it, I don't allow rejection to rent room in my head and neither should you.

I won't lie to you, an acceptance would be great – but it's not the end of the world if it doesn't happen. I know now that a story might not land with a publisher or call for many differing reasons but whatever those reasons may be, ***don't let it steal your joy of writing*** because it can, and it often does.

In the following notes I'll try and give you some insight into each of the stories in this, my debut collection and how they came to be.

Thank you for reading 'Beautiful Atrocities' and I hope you find the following notes insightful.

One Piece Remains

One Piece Remains was written for the horror anthology 'What One Wouldn't Do" which was edited by Scott. J. Moses. As soon as I'd heard about the theme I was desperate to get a story in this anthology. I'd also seen on social media some of the names floating around, those talented writers who were submitting a story and I'd thought to myself 'I'd give my right arm to be included in that' - but alas, I received a rejection. After sending One Piece Remains to a few trusted friends/writers and seeing that the story did indeed work, I decided to put it front and centre. I couldn't think of a better story to open my collection. I think it's a great tone setter.

When It Is Truly Time

This story has been floating around for a while in my head and I just needed something to hang it from. One day I was watching an advert on TV about a cancer charity and then my mind clicked and the opening of the story fell into place. I decided to set the story out as if it were a chemotherapy clinic but instead of injecting poison into their veins, they were instead injecting the ghost of their loved ones. I also think that the premise of this story is going to take the form of a longer story in the not too distant future.

\<TheCollectorOfRuinedThings\>

As with many of my short works (and with some of my longer work) I like to flip things on their heads and this one came to me in the moment when I was drifting off to sleep. I'd been wanting to write a story in a morgue for a long time, but I didn't want it to be overtly obvious; I wanted to deploy a sleight of hand if you will, and when that element found me as I was drifting off to sleep I knew I had the missing piece of the puzzle. To say I wasn't influenced by Eric LaRocca's 'Things Have Gotten Worse Since We Last Spoke' would be an understatement - this story is almost a love song to that beautiful book and wonderful author.

All The Little Children

I tend to find myself on numerous occasions scrolling through Twitter on a regular basis when I should be writing. I won't be too harsh on myself because the idea for this story fell into my lap on one such occasion. One of the most disturbing images I'd seen in a while popped onto my screen of a realistic, knitted baby. It was utterly hideous, a ghastly thing that I couldn't shake. It would have been a travesty not to write a story from such a prompt. This one was also written during the lockdowns that followed Covid when all of us thought it would be for a few weeks and ended up sticking around a bit longer than that. In the UK at a certain time in the night on a certain day, everyone would stand on their doorsteps and clap the NHS and this theme also played into the story.

Cuckoo, Cuckoo, Cuckoo

There's not much to tell about this one. I've always been fascinated with nature and when I read about the Cuckoo and what it does to survive, I just sat down with an open word document and this tale appeared on the page. I was also writing 'Only The Stains Remain' during this time and so the acts of torture and revenge were filling my waking moments, so I feel a little bit of that bled into this story.

A Place To Lay Me Down

As well as a morgue setting, I've always wanted to tell a story of a gravedigger / graveyard and this one was a pure joy to write. My good friends Tony Self and Tomek Dzido (amazing writers in their own right and the dearest of friends) and I had been writing a story a week from January 2021 to July 2021. We would set ourselves a title and each of us would go away and write a short story to that title. That particular week it was 'Reserved' and so I used that as my fuel and began crafting this tale of death and the grave. I'd seen a picture a few weeks before getting this prompt of a grave and a sign with an arrow pointing down into it. You can't make this up, the word on the sign was 'Reserved'.

Hail Maud Full of Grace

As people read my work, they will soon realise that I like to use my small platform to write about deeply challenging issues. For example 'Tome' focusses on racism, 'Juniper' domestic abuse and loneliness, 'Only The Stains Remain' child abuse and 'Tethered' toxic masculinity. Hail Maud Full of Grace came to me at a time when I had been seeing lots of reports and court cases about police brutality and the murdering of innocent individual at their hand. I had to write it, I felt compelled to write it and so I did. I hope it resonates with the reader.

Mortal Wound

I wanted to tell a story of a life that had been broken apart by circumstance and told in an interesting style. I had a picture of a woman crying, weeping her heart out under a willow. Then one night I remember thinking about my first kiss with my wife and I could remember it all. Then I began to wonder if memories could be stored in kisses (like little time capsules) and that idea formed the structure of this piece.

Trapped In The Amber Of This Moment

This story was originally written at a flash fiction retreat in Bristol which I was attending to learn about how to write a novella in flash (which turned out to be Tethered). The workshop consisted of us closing our eyes and listening to someone set the scene for our story. They spoke about place, and smell and sounds etc. Then we had a short time to craft something after she'd finished talking. It was an interesting exercise and I loved this piece of flash and wanted to include it in the collection. Horror Oasis have an audio version of this story on their YouTube account where it's called Mosquito - go give it a listen, it's great.

Casualties of War

I've always been fascinated with trauma and more importantly the trauma of war. I am also deeply grateful for all those soldiers who fight for our freedoms, but lose themselves or pieces of themselves on the battlefield. It was my way of highlighting the concept of what we lose when we fight, and what the mind of the soldier brings back with them from war and the scars that never heal.

Heads That Could Shatter Glass

I'd liked the idea of a man being held captive by his child with no way out. I've been in that dark place before, where you just want your baby to stop crying, but you're powerless to stop them. In that moment you'd literally do anything to stop that soul shredding scream - luckily I didn't resort to the same fix as our protagonist. Brian Bowyer made me do it!

Cat Box

This was written for the submission call from Gabino Iglesias and Andrew Cull for their an anthology of Lost Footage. I really enjoyed coming up with the premise for this one, trying to steer away from the usual conventions of found footage films etc. I think I managed it and Cat Box was created – now I'm scared a video will appear on my doorstep any day now.

The Yellow Man and His Insatiable Hunger

This story is probably the most personal story I've written in this collection. Trudy in this story was based on one of my own relatives and I hated every moment we were at her house. Everything from the sandwiches to the chocolate, to the wooden leg and the coins. Who needs nightmares when the waking day and childhoods are full of possibilities. Much later in her life when we visited her in Brighton, I watched on as she talked on a CB radio to the boats out her window. She told us on that visit about these large, yellow balls that were eating her head. She'd said they came out at night to feast on her mind. Bless her, she's dead now but her nightmares are now mine and yours.

Even Death Can't Separate Us

I've had an idea of writing a circus freak story for quite some time. I think ever since I watched *that* episode of The X-Files. It was written in the stars long ago and all I needed was an excuse to write it. Well it's taken me a while, but I managed it and to the keen eyed reader and dare I say it fans of my work; may have noticed a little mention of a crazy town. If so, this story has kindled a fire in me to write a short story collection about Juniper at some point, stories about some of the lives I've touched upon who didn't get the page time they rightly deserved.

The Great Withering

When I was approached by Keith Anthony Baird to help edit and contribute a story to Hex-Periments a charity anthology raising funds for The Bristol Methodist Centre (a homeless day centre) I jumped at the chance. This story is going to form a much larger piece, a novel I think, which will focus on the central themes of this snapshot of a future in ruin. I'm excited about it and can't wait to add a little of my blend of horror to the world of dystopian fiction!

A Distant Silence

This flash fiction piece was more of an exercise for me. I wanted to see if I could successfully manage to tell a haunting story in the space of only a few words. I find it creepy, and I wanted to include it because the premise scared me the more I thought about it.

Two Beasts, One Master

If you've read my book Tethered you'll know I have a few things to say about toxic masculinity. This was another story that was written for an anthology call – *Dead Inside* - alas it didn't make the cut but I loved the depiction in this story of toxic masculinity so much that I had to include it in my collection. I feel it's powerful and also shows that if we bury this stuff, if we hold on to past hurts we'll eventually pass it on to our children.

Beautiful Atrocities

I needed a title story for this collection and so I sat down, drank some coffee and just opened a word document. I had no idea where it would go, or what it would become. This was an experiment in just letting the story take me and writing without any restrictions. It's the weirdest story in the collection I think, but one I loved writing. I also wanted to shine a light on domestic violence and put a spin on it, because a lot of people often forget that men also suffer from domestic abuse and it's a lot more common than one might think.

So, that's it.

You got to peek behind the curtain. I hope it didn't disappoint, and I also hope you'll be back for more short story collections in the future and also more of my lengthier works.

Thank you for picking up Beautiful Atrocities when there are so many other books vying for your time, money and attention.

If you enjoyed this book please do consider leaving a review on Amazon, Goodreads, Instagram, YouTube and Twitter because as an indie author I can honestly tell you that word of mouth; and reviews really do help a book get more attention.

Thank you!

About the Author

Ross Jeffery is the Bram Stoker and 3x Splatterpunk Award-nominated author of Tome, Juniper, Only the Stains Remain, Milk Kisses & Other Stories and Tethered.

He is a Bristol based writer and *Executive Director of* STORGY Magazine. Ross has appeared in many print publications and has a great deal of work in online literary journals.

Ross lives in Bristol with his wife (Anna) and two children (Eva and Sophie).

You can follow him on Twitter @RossJeffery_

CONTENT WARNING
CONTINUED

Hail Maud Full of Grace - Racism

Cat Box - Child Death

The Great Withering - Experimentation on Children, Physical Abuse

Trapped In The Amber of This Moment - Domestic Abuse

Beautiful Atrocities - Domestic Abuse

Cuckoo, Cuckoo, Cuckoo - Torture

A Place To Lay Me Down - Buried Alive

Heads That Could Shatter Glass - Vehicular Homicide

Two Beasts, One Master - Toxic Masculinity

Casualties of War - Trauma & Injury Detail

Made in the USA
Middletown, DE
23 May 2022

66104526R00104